Trouble in Contrary Woods

A Bailey Fish Adventure

Linda Salisbury

Drawings by Carol Tornatore

Tabby House

Cover design and illustrations: Carol Tornatore
Author photo: Elaine Taylor

Library of Congress Cataloging-in-Publication Data

Salisbury, Linda G. (Linda Grotke)
Trouble in Contrary Woods : a Bailey Fish adventure /
Linda Salisbury ; drawings by Carol Tornatore.
    p. cm.
Includes book club questions, glossary, and related web
sites.
Summary: When Bailey's cousin Duck arrives for a visit,
Bailey is dismayed to discover that he is afraid of bugs
and does not like the outdoors, but a few weeks of adven-
tures looking for a bear, translating mysterious messages
left on a tree stump, and creating inventions help Duck
stop worrying so much and enjoy his visit.
ISBN-13: 978-1-881539-46-9
ISBN-10: 1-881539-46-6
[1. Cousins--Fiction. 2. Worry--Fiction. 3. Inventions--Fic-
tion. 4. Dogs--Fiction. 5. Country life--Virginia--Fiction. 6.
Grandmothers--Fiction.] I. Tornatore, Carol, ill. II. Title.
PZ7.S1524Tr 2009
[Fic]--dc22
                                    2008027108

baileyfish@gmail.com
www.BaileyFishAdventures.com
www.BaileyFishAdventureBooks.blogspot/com

Classroom quantities available.

Tabby House
P.O. Box 544, Mineral, VA 23117

(540) 894-8868

Contents

1
Giant Mess

"Sugar, come quick! Something terrible has happened!" Bailey Fish stared in disbelief at her grandmother's yard. Birdhouses and bird feeders were strewn everywhere. One section of the white picket fence around the vegetable garden was smashed, as if a giant foot had stomped on it.

Bailey cautiously opened the screen door. She put her hand in her new dog's blue collar and stepped out on the back porch. She squinted in the morning sunlight. All the apples were stripped from a small tree.

Her dog growled softly.

"What is it, girl?" whispered Bailey. The hound whimpered and tried to pull away toward the woods.

Bailey's grandmother pushed open the screen door. "Oh, my goodness," Sugar said. "What a mess!"

"Who did it, Sugar?" asked Bailey.

"Let's have a look," said her grandmother. "Get a leash for your dog so that she doesn't take off running."

Sugar slipped on her old brown moccasins that were shiny with years of wear, and Bailey hooked the leash on Dog's collar. She had owned Dog for only a few days and hadn't yet decided on a permanent name for her. The woman who had been caring for Dog called her "Angel." Bailey liked that name okay, but she wasn't sure it was the perfect name. So she just called her "Dog."

Dog strained at the end of her leash and tugged Bailey toward the woods. "Oh, no, you don't," Bailey said. She held the leash tighter.

"Hmmm," said Sugar. She picked up the bluebird houses and examined them. "Looks like this little nest is ruined. And, look, the eggs fell out of that one. Poor parents."

Sugar scooped up the cracked hummingbird feeder and studied it. "Just as I thought." She gazed at the woods.

"What is it?" asked Bailey.

"Bear. I believe the culprit is a hungry black bear," said her grandmother.

"A bear? How can you tell?" Bailey looked around to make sure the bear wasn't creeping up behind them. In all her eleven years she had never seen a live bear, except in a zoo.

"Teeth marks and other evidence. Bears like apples, birdseed, and the sweet sugar mixture in the hummingbird feeders. We'll have to take the feeders that aren't broken into the toolshed at night."

"Won't the bear get us?" asked Bailey. She was a worrier, and this was something new and big to worry about.

"I don't think we need to be afraid, unless she has a cub. We'll just take away temptation by removing food. Meantime, perhaps you'll see the bear walking through the yard one of these nights or mornings."

"Wait till I tell everyone," said Bailey. "A real bear. That's so awesome." She was relieved that Dog had stopped pulling and was now sitting down with her tail wagging. Then Dog lifted her nose and sniffed.

"Maybe Dog barked at five this morning because of the bear. She woke me up," said Bailey, looking around again.

She knelt down and hugged the hound. Dog trembled happily and leaned into her. Bailey's hand slid over a silky tan ear.

"That's why we adopted her." Sugar smiled. "You wanted a dog for protection."

Bailey still wasn't really sure why her grandmother had changed her mind and agreed to let Bailey have Dog. It really didn't matter.

Off Bailey and Sugar had gone just a week ago in the red pickup to have a look at the abandoned dog, a tall, graceful Walker hound-mix with a long tail, soft ears, and spots of white, black, and tan. One spot on her neck was gold.

Mrs. Chaffee, the woman who rescued the dog, said Angel barked when strangers were around, but the dog made no sound when Bailey and Sugar knocked on Mrs. Chaffee's front door. The dog seemed shy, but happily left with Bailey after she petted her and gave her a biscuit.

When they got home, Bailey spread blankets on the floor near her bed, where she could reach down and stroke her new friend. The dog climbed up in her bed in the middle of the night and put her head on Bailey's pillow. Bailey's young cats, Shadow and Sallie, were not pleased. They curled up on her chair and hissed when Dog got off the bed the next morning. Dog ignored them.

"You're so pretty. Good girl," whispered Bailey to the dog. "I know Shadow and Sallie will like you soon. They lived here first and they don't know you."

Now, a week later, the cats were still hissing, but not quite so much.

"I'm going back inside to have my coffee," said Sugar, "and to get out of my PJs. I'd keep your dog leashed until after breakfast. We don't want her chasing off into the woods now that we know a bear is out there."

"Okay," said Bailey. She sat on the damp grass, and Dog lay down and put her head in her lap. Bailey stroked her soft fur. She had never before owned a dog, just cats, a gerbil named Gert, and a hermit crab named Hairy-Berry.

When she lived in Florida, before her mother, Molly, went to work in Costa Rica, Bailey's cat, Barker, had been run over. Then Bailey came to live with her grandmother during the winter, and Sugar let her get kittens. Bailey had no idea how long she would be staying with Sugar, and there seemed to be less and less talk of Molly returning anytime soon.

Dog lifted her head and sniffed the air again. She growled. The hair on her neck raised. Bailey heard the snapping of brush in the woods.

"Let's get out of here," she said to Dog. She ran to the house, dragging the hound behind her.

2

Unexpected Cousin

Sugar was dressed in her denim work clothes and drinking black coffee when Bailey and Dog dashed through the door.

"Sugar, we just heard something in the woods. I was going to go to Keswick Inn this morning. Do you think it's safe to walk over?"

"I should think so. Mr. Bear is likely sleeping during the day. He's probably more afraid of you than you are of him. But I'll go with you if you want me to."

"Thanks," said Bailey. "Dog acts like there's something out there."

"She was trained as a hunter," said Sugar. "Her keen nose detects something. Might be deer. Might be a rabbit."

"Or a bear," said Bailey. She gave the dog a bone-shaped biscuit and filled her water bowl.

"By the way, I've got news," said her grandmother.

Bailey scooped pieces of kibble into Dog's dish, then looked up.

"I don't know if you remember me talking about my cousin, Max Keller. He has a grandson, Duck—that's what they call him. Duck's about your age, and they'd like to have him visit for a while."

"Visit us?" asked Bailey. She didn't remember hearing about Sugar's cousin, Max Keller. Besides, her mind was still on the bear.

"Yes, us," said Sugar. "Duck's grown up in a city and has had a hard time. Cousin Max thought it would be nice for him to have a few weeks in the country."

Bailey's mind churned. "When's Duck coming? Where will he sleep?"

"I had a call late last night, and, well, he's coming sooner than I expected. I was so distracted by the bear's damage this morning that I forgot to tell you. Duck'll be here today. This afternoon. I figure he can sleep in the guest room."

"Is he my *real* cousin?" Bailey asked. She shoved her straight, medium-brown hair behind her ears. "I didn't know I had a cousin."

"Yes, but not a first cousin. You would have a first cousin if your mother had a brother or sister who had a child. Molly's an only child."

Bailey poured oat cereal into a bowl. She asked, "Why do they call him Duck?"

"It's because of the first initials of his four names," said Sugar. "I'll let you ask Duck what they are."

Bailey's hazel eyes widened. She had never heard of anyone having four names. "Okay," she said, even though she wanted Sugar to tell her.

"Now, as soon as you finish your cereal, please put clean towels on the guest bed, and then we'll go over to see the Keswicks," said Sugar.

"I wonder if the bear visited them last night, too," said Bailey.

"We'll find out," said Sugar.

3

Sparrow's Fear

The Keswick boys were inside the house helping their mother clean the guest rooms when Bailey and Sugar arrived.

Sparrow, the boys' seven-year-old foster sister, was wiping off chairs on the front porch. Sparrow had parked her wheelchair close to the chairs so she could reach them with her bucket and big yellow sponge. Bailey knew that Sparrow didn't like being in the wheelchair. Her doctors said that the little girl's hips would eventually heal, but in the meantime, she couldn't walk for at least a year. A year was a long time.

The Keswicks' dog, Clover, jumped off Sparrow's lap and ran to Bailey and Dog.

"Guess what? We had a bear in our yard last night," said Bailey. "And I have a cousin coming later today." She grabbed a sponge to help Sparrow wipe the taller chairs.

"You have a cousin who's a bear?" said Sparrow.

"No, a cousin cousin. His name is Duck," said Bailey.

"That's funny. A duck cousin," said Sparrow, giggling. "Will you fix my hair? It's getting in my eyes."

Bailey pulled the strands of Sparrow's dark blond hair into a ponytail.

"I don't remember if I have cousins," said Sparrow, "except foster ones." She reached down to pet Bailey's dog.

Sparrow rarely talked about her birth family. She had lived in foster homes most of her life.

"I didn't know I had a cousin, either," said Bailey.

"Do you like him?" Sparrow asked.

"I'm sure we'll like him a lot," Bailey said.

"Oh." Sparrow wiped her soapy hands on her jeans. "Bailey, are you ever scared?"

"Sure," said Bailey.

"I'm scared of the woods," said Sparrow.

"Why?"

"There are things that might get me and I can't run," said Sparrow. "I'm supposed to stay in this stupid chair until my hips heal even though I could walk if the doctors let me."

"If your legs work, I'm sure the Keswicks would understand if you had to run for just a minute to save yourself," said Bailey.

"What about the bear?" asked Sparrow.

"When I'm scared, here's what Sugar told me to do. First, I pretend the thing I'm afraid of is shrinking. I imagine it gets smaller and smaller until it's small enough to put in my pocket. I can keep it there, but it's not big enough to scare me all the time."

"Really?" said Sparrow. "I could pretend the bear is in my pocket. That'd be silly."

"That's what I'd do," said Bailey. "Now, if you're done with the chairs, where's that book you wanted to read to me?"

Sparrow said, "Here." She pulled *Good Work, Amelia Bedelia* from a pouch in her wheelchair. "This is really funny. I'll read it to you—after I put the bear in my pocket." She grinned.

Bailey sat down on a damp chair next to Sparrow and watched over the girl's shoulder. Sparrow turned the pages and read, sounding out words that were unfamiliar.

"You're doing great," Bailey told her.

4

Cousin Duck

Bailey and Sugar walked back home shortly before company arrived.

Cousin Duck was not at all like Bailey expected. He was shorter and thinner, had solemn blue eyes, and thick, short reddish-brown hair that rippled like waves on his head. His wire-rim glasses balanced on his pug nose, and he had dimples in his cheeks.

She was most surprised that, even in the midsummer heat, Cousin Duck wore a freshly pressed white shirt buttoned to his throat, navy slacks with a belt, and polished brown loafers. Bailey opened the screen door and he stuck out his hand.

"You must be Bailey," Duck said stiffly, as if he had arrived at a party for the president of the United States.

"Hi," she said, feeling odd about calling him by his nickname.

"I'm Duck," the boy said, as if it were a normal name like Bob or John. He stared at Bailey.

"Hey, Max," Sugar called from the side yard. Bailey saw a stocky man with gray hair put down a black suitcase and give Sugar a hug.

"Long time no see," he said. "Much too long. I can't tell you how grateful I am that you'll take Duck for a couple of weeks. I hope he isn't too much of a challenge. I know your granddaughter's already living here."

"We'll be just fine. Let me give you the tour of my humble country estate." Sugar laughed.

"I'd love to see your place," said Duck's grandfather.

Duck and Bailey stood uncomfortably in the front hall. "Where will I be staying?" he asked.

"Upstairs. Follow me," said Bailey. Dog raced up the stairs ahead of her. Duck clomped behind them. She led him down the hall to the guest room with a single bed and a small desk and chair.

"Where's the computer? I don't see a TV or CD player," Duck said. He looked around the room.

"We don't have any stuff like that in the bedrooms," said Bailey. "Just downstairs."

Duck scowled. "What am I supposed to do then?"

"We go outside a lot," said Bailey. "There's always neat things to do. I'll take you to Keswick Inn and you can meet everybody—all my friends."

"I don't want to meet anybody. I'm not staying long. I'll ask Grandfather to get a computer set up in my room. I like to play games and check things on the Internet." Duck shoved his hands in his pockets.

"What's this about a computer?" asked Cousin Max. He carried Duck's suitcase into the room. "You're going to pretty much have to live without one during your stay. Sugar only has dial-up and one computer in her office. You can use the computer only when she gives permission."

"Then I'm not staying," said Duck. He grabbed the handle of his suitcase and dragged it toward the bedroom door.

"Not an option," said his grandfather. "Your grandmother needs medical treatment in St. Louis, and we can't take you with us. You'll have a good time here. Now give me a hug and make the best of things. Chin up." His grandfather reached out his arms. Duck turned his back. "I want to be alone, sir," he said.

His grandfather looked like he wanted to hug the boy. Instead he sighed and said, "I'll call you soon, buddy." He waited a minute, then left the room with Bailey.

Duck shut his bedroom door. Hard.

"Hmmm," said Sugar, when Bailey and Duck's grandfather came downstairs. "Do you have time for iced tea, Max?"

He looked at his watch. "I guess so. Thanks. I'm sorry about Duck's rudeness. He was a cheery little fellow until he had to come live with us in the city a couple of years ago. Since his grandmother became ill, she worries about him all the time and is rather overprotective. He stays indoors so much in the city that he hasn't made many friends, and well, he seems to have forgotten how to play and just have fun. He's really smart. I hope you can help him, Bailey."

Bailey nodded, but she wasn't sure it was going to work, especially if Duck sulked forever in his room. She had no plans to stay home and watch TV just because he didn't want to go outside. There was too much to do with her friends.

Sparrow wanted to practice reading with her. Miss Bekka said she would show Bailey how to make blackberry cobbler. And almost every afternoon everyone went for a swim in the lake.

Bailey looked around for Dog. She wasn't in the living room or the kitchen. Bailey went back upstairs. Dog was curled up outside the guest bedroom door.

"There you are," said Bailey. "I've been looking all over for you."

The hound thumped her tail and put her head down.

"See if you can make Duck feel at home," said Bailey. She went back downstairs to help Sugar with supper.

5

City Boy

"Glad you decided to join us," said Sugar. Duck and Dog appeared just as Sugar took the tilapia off the grill. "Your grandfather said you like fish."

"It's healthy," said Duck with a stony face. "I always order it at restaurants. We go out almost every night. The waiters know what I like."

"We don't go to restaurants much around here, except for burger night," said Sugar. "We're pretty far out in the country."

Duck looked at the kitchen clock. "May I please use your computer after supper?" he asked. He nibbled at his fish.

"Sure, but I must go over the computer rules with you. In my house, I need to see what sites you are looking at, and I want to be able to check your e-mail from time to time. We can all learn a lot from the Internet. It's a great way to communicate, but kids need to be safe. Agreed?"

Duck nodded yes. "I have the same rules at home," he said.

"Good," said Sugar. "Now, you can use the Internet for fifteen minutes, then it'll be Bailey's turn for fifteen, and then we'll sit out on the porch and read and look at lightning bugs and stars," said Sugar.

"I don't like bugs. Don't you watch TV?" Duck asked.

"Not much," said Sugar. "We like books and—"

"And wild animals," interrupted Bailey. "If we're lucky, we might see the bear tonight."

Duck's fork froze in midair, as if he were ready to defend himself. His pale blue eyes widened. "A bear?"

"We have one in the neighborhood," said Sugar. "It's been raiding our bird feeders."

"Aren't you going to get rid of it?" Duck asked.

"Oh, my, no! We moved into bear habitat. We must learn to coexist," said Sugar.

Duck shook his head in disbelief. "I think you should shoot it or trap it," he said, trying to sound brave. He aimed his fork at the window. "I could make you a bear-shooting machine."

"We *like* nature," said Bailey quickly. Why would Duck want to kill the bear? What was the matter with him? She hadn't really liked Duck when she met him. Then she felt a little sorry for him, but now she didn't like him at all.

Duck finished his meal in silence and asked Sugar again about using her computer.

"After you help with the dishes," said Sugar.

Duck said, "I don't do dishes. Grandmother has a lady who does that."

"In my house, everyone helps," said Sugar with a kind smile. "I'll wash, you dry, and Bailey will put things away."

Duck looked like he was about to object, but then got up and helped clear the table. Sugar smiled again and said, "Dish towels are in the top drawer next to the sink."

6

E-mail for Bailey

Bailey listened for the computer tones that signaled that the dial-up connection was being made to the Internet.

"Gee, this takes forever," Duck said to Sugar.

"We have to have patience in the country," said Sugar. "Maybe someday we'll have high-speed Internet like you do in the city."

Bailey watched from the doorway while Sugar showed Duck how to use her computer. He quickly became frustrated with how long everything was taking and said he was done.

When he went up to his room, Bailey checked her e-mail.

There was one from her mother.

From: Mollyf2@travl.net
To: "Bailey"<baileyfish@gmail.com>
Sent: 2:30 p.m.
Subject: Trip

Bails, sweetie, Andrew and I went to the mountain town of Sarchi yesterday to see the famous beautifully painted ox carts and wooden furniture. Local artists paint them with flowers and all sorts of fabulous designs. Andrew's friends received a decorative ox cart as a wedding present. They use it in their living room to hold books and magazines. Here's a picture of the painted tray I bought for Sugar. I'm also sending her money for your new school clothes. You'll probably want to go shopping soon. Wish I was there to go to the mall with you. XXXOOO, Mom

Sarchi tray.jpg

Bailey stared at the computer screen without replying. She was sick of her mother talking about this Dr. Andrew Snorge-Swinson. She wanted her mother to e-mail her that she had finished writing her book about his work as an entomologist. If her mom liked shopping with her so much, why wasn't she coming home to buy school clothes with her?

Bailey's hand gripped the mouse and her neck stiffened. She tried to remember her mother's soft skin and thick dark hair and how her laugh made Bailey feel like every day was a holiday. She wished that Bug Man, as she called Dr. Andrew Snorge-Swinson, had been trampled by an ox in Sarchi, or carried off by a giant insect that he was studying.

She clicked open the next message. It was from her father in Guam. She had met him for the first time a few months earlier when he stopped by with her half sister, Norma Jean. He e-mailed at least once a week. Sometimes he asked questions she didn't feel like answering, such as what was going on with her mother.

From: pjfish2005@yermail.net>
To: "Bailey"<baileyfish@gmail.com>
Sent: 5:15 p.m.
Subject: hey there

Dear Bailey: I'm still working on getting a job in the States and have several good leads. Norma Jean is really looking forward to spending more time with you. Flora and the boys can't wait to meet you. I found another clarinet duet for us to play. It's an arrangement of "My Country 'Tis of Thee." We can do a patriotic concert together.

What do you hear from your mom? Does she have plans to return? Does she want you to live with her in Costa Rica? Dad

Bailey deleted his message without answering. She heard Sugar inviting Duck to come back down to sit on the porch. He said he was going to read in his room where there weren't bugs or animals.

"I'm coming, Sugar," said Bailey. She logged off and turned out the office light.

7

Not Curious

Sugar dropped off Bailey, Duck, and Dog at Keswick Inn on her way to town to get the mail. "Have fun," she said. "I'll see you back at the house for lunch."

Bailey worried that her friends would think Duck was weird when they saw him in his ironed white shirt, clean navy slacks, white socks, and brown loafers. He certainly wasn't dressed for adventure in the country. Plus, Duck looked miserable, like he had been forced to eat slimy fruit cocktail instead of his favorite ice cream.

"C'mon," Bailey said. Dog strained at her leash, but Duck was in no hurry. He scuffed along behind her. Bailey waved at Miss Bekka, who was sweeping the inn's porch.

"The boys and Sparrow are out back by the chicken coop," called Miss Bekka. "Welcome, Duck. We hope you'll like it here. Just call me

Miss Bekka, and my husband, Mr. Will. It's a Southern thing." She smiled warmly and pulled her long, blond braid over her shoulder.

"Yes, ma'am," Duck said flatly.

"Are the Phiggs here today?" asked Bailey.

"No, they've gone to Jamestown for a week or so to do research on Elmo's book," said Miss Bekka. "Keswick Inn is without guests."

"Oh," said Bailey. "Everybody's away. Emily and her family are camping near Luray Caverns. I got a postcard yesterday."

Bailey saw Sparrow waving. Forgetting about pokey Duck, she dropped the leash and sprinted with Dog past the big barn to the chicken coop.

Noah and Fred were bent over fastening chicken-wire to a fence post. Sparrow was sitting in her wheelchair with Clover in her lap. The Keswicks' little fluffy white dog jumped down and dashed at Dog. Clover rolled at Dog's feet, wanting to play. Dog pushed her with her nose, and off they went on a chase through the orchard.

"We had a bear visit us last night," said Sparrow. "Look what he did to the apple tree."

Bailey saw that a low, thin branch was broken off, and all the apples were gone.

"It might be the same bear that smashed our bird feeders," said Bailey. The boys looked past her at Duck, who was slowly wandering closer.

"That your cousin?" asked Noah.

"My sort-of cousin," said Bailey. She wished Duck would try to be friendlier so that the boys would like him, but Duck looked bored.

"This is Duck," she said.

"That's a funny name," said Sparrow.

"Dabney Unger Carr Keller. If you take the first initials of each they spell 'Duck,' " said Duck, without smiling.

"How did you get so many names?" asked Sparrow.

"Nobody in the family could agree, so they gave me all the names they liked," said Duck. "Go ahead and laugh. Everyone does."

No one laughed. Instead, they looked puzzled.

"Well," said Fred, introducing himself and his brother. "We're the twins, and this is our foster sister, Sparrow."

Bailey smiled at their joke. She had planned to tell Duck about the "twins" before they went to the Keswicks', but he hadn't seemed interested in knowing about her friends.

If Duck had been at all curious, she would have told him that Fred and Noah were both twelve and adopted. Noah's parents died when he was a baby, and he was adopted by his uncle, Will Keswick. Fred was also adopted as a baby. Noah looked like Mr. Will. He had unruly hair the color of a yellow cat, and greenish eyes just like his uncle.

Fred, however, was brown-skinned, with almost-black curly hair. Bailey heard that the Keswicks wanted to adopt Sparrow, too, but she didn't know if that would happen.

Maybe Duck would be curious about Bailey's friends on the way back to Sugar's house. Bailey had lots to tell him about everyone if he wanted to know.

"Twins?" Duck looked surprised. He glanced at the boys, then at Bailey.

"Yes," said Noah, with a straight face. "Twins."

"Oh," said Duck. He walked over to a pear tree and broke small twigs off the branches.

8

Naming Dog

"So when are you going to give Dog a real name?" asked Fred. He tossed a biscuit to the spindly hound. His little muffy white dog jumped up to try and grab it from Dog's mouth. Dog turned her head away. "Here's one for you, Clover," said Fred. He broke a biscuit in half and tossed it to her.

"I'm working on it," said Bailey. "My cats' names were easy, but a good one for Dog is harder. I've never had a dog."

"We'll help," said Noah. "Make a list, bro," he said to Fred.

Fred grabbed his yellow pad and pencil. "Bailey, you start," he said.

"Okay," said Bailey. "We don't know what the hunter called her before he abandoned her in the woods. Sugar said she probably wasn't a good deer hunter. Mrs. Chaffee called her Angel. Angel's all right, but—"

"But she's your dog now," said Sparrow. "I think you should call her Tippy. She has a white tip on her tail."

Bailey said, "I was thinking of Peaches or Emma." She stroked Dog's tan ears. Dog thumped her long brown tail with the white tip.

"She looks like she has a huge white leaf on her back," said Noah. "Name her Leaffy." Fred wrote down Angel, Dog, Tippy, Peaches, Emma, and Leaffy.

"What about you? Any ideas, Duck?" asked Fred.

Duck stood stiffly next to the Chicken Coop Theater while the others lounged on the freshly mowed grass. He ran his hand through his hair. "Nope. I never named a dog."

"Do you have any pets?" asked Sparrow.

"I had a turtle when I was little. I have a betta fish now."

"What's its name?" asked Sparrow.

"Wolf," answered Duck. "I call him Wolfie."

"That's a funny name for a fish," said Sparrow. She rolled her chair closer to him and brushed her long bangs out of her face.

"No, it's not," said Duck. "I tap on the side of his glass bowl and call, 'Wolfie,' and he comes."

"Really?" said Sparrow pushing her hair behind her ears. She sounded like she wasn't sure she should believe him.

"Really," said Duck. Bailey thought she saw his lips twitch into a slight smile.

The twins said nothing. Fred studied his list. "What other ideas do we have?" he asked. "You haven't suggested a name, dude."

"Dogwinkle," his brother said.

"Huh?" said Fred.

"Think about it," said Noah. "Dogwinkle is a type of shell, and Bailey comes from Florida where there are tons of shells."

"Or Sanibel," said Sparrow. "She always talks about Sanibel beaches, right, Bailey?"

Fred added Sanibel to his list of Good Names for Dog. He chewed on the tip of his pencil. "How about Helena?"

Dog sighed and rolled on her side.

"This is stupid," said Duck. "I thought we were going to *do* something today."

He broke off another small branch from the pear tree and snapped it in half. He then slapped at his sleeve and stumbled backwards. "Get it away. Someone help me!" Duck begged.

No one moved. "I mean it. What on earth is that thing?" Duck brushed at his arm and stomped his feet.

Bailey stood up and walked over to her cousin. "It's just a daddy longlegs," she said. "They don't bite."

Duck didn't look convinced. He examined his shirtsleeves and flicked off a piece of bark. "Can we go now, Bailey?" he pleaded.

Bailey was torn. Duck was sort of her guest, but she didn't want to leave her friends while they were helping her name the dog, and he was being such a whiny baby about everything. She looked at Fred, "Another name I've been thinking about is Celeste."

Fred wrote it down.

"Please?" begged Duck.

Bailey stood up. "All right. C'mon, Dog," she said. "See ya," she called to her friends. If Duck didn't like the wildlife in the Keswicks' yard, he surely wouldn't like walking home through the woods where there were even more bugs and spiderwebs.

9

Yard Sale Treasures

"So, what *do* you like to do?" Bailey asked. She jumped over a muddy streambed. Duck stopped, apparently trying to figure out how to get across without getting his leather shoes muddy.

"Lots of things," he said. "Computers and games. I invent things. Dang!" His jump to the other side landed him in reddish squishy muck. "Oh, man, Grandmother will be mad!"

"Why? It's just mud," said Bailey.

"You don't know my grandmother," said Duck. "She has a fit if I spill anything or get dirty."

"I'm lucky. Sugar's not that way. We always have dirt on our clothes from being outside. Hey, what do you invent?" asked Bailey. Duck looked surprised that she was interested.

"I made a rocket ship once when I was five. It didn't fly, so I turned it into a race car. When it didn't drive, I took it apart and made a book-shelf. Stuff like that."

"Do you still make things?" Bailey asked.

"I don't have my workbench anymore. Grandmother's afraid I might hurt myself with a saw or hammer. So, mostly I draw my inventions. I know they would work if I could just make them."

"Could you draw one for me?" asked Bailey.

"Sure," said Duck. Sugar's house was now in view. Dog bolted after a squirrel, then happily returned to Bailey after the squirrel streaked up a hickory tree. It chattered angrily from a high branch.

"Silly girl," said Bailey, rubbing Dog's ears.

When they reached the yard, they saw Sugar kneeling next to several cartons on her porch. She picked up a book and blew off dust.

"Back so soon?" she asked when she heard Bailey and Duck come up the wooden steps.

Bailey decided not to say anything about Duck not wanting to help name the dog or about the daddy longlegs. She said simply, "Duck got mud on his shoes. He needs to change."

Sugar said, "Well, now. I think our guest needs country clothes. I stopped at a yard sale this morning down the road and found things in his size. Take this box upstairs, Duck, and see what fits you for country living."

Duck hesitated. He opened the box. "The clothes are used." He scowled.

"Best kind for being outside. Won't matter if they get dirty or torn," said Sugar. She continued to unpack the books.

"But . . ." said Duck.

"Suit yourself," said Sugar. Her back was still turned to him. Duck hesitated, then picked up the box and went inside. The door slapped closed behind him.

"How's it going?" Sugar asked Bailey.

"He doesn't like anything or anybody very much," said Bailey.

"Give him time," said her grandmother.

"I am. What's in the boxes?"

"Have a look. Lots of children's books. Mostly old ones. Ones I remember from when I was a girl. The Bobbsey Twins. Nancy Drew. The Hardy Boys. Jerry Todd. Dr. Doolittle. They're parts of series. I loved reading series, especially in the summer when I had lots of time. Would you and your friends be interested in them?"

"Sure," said Bailey. She smiled when she saw the title *Jerry Todd and the Purring Egg.* She opened it to find out how an egg could purr.

"Books?" asked Duck through the screen door. Bailey saw that he was now wearing jeans and a red T-shirt and the maroon sneakers with holes in the toes.

"Do you have any Edgar Allan Poe?" Duck asked.

"I'm not sure what's in the boxes, but I have Poe in my library," Sugar said. "I'll show you."

"I'd like that," said Duck.

10

Afraid of Everything

"Ouch. Ouch," grumbled Duck as he followed Bailey and Dog back to Keswick Inn. He was wearing his new used clothes. Tucked under his arm was a frayed red towel with a bathing suit wrapped in it. The Keswicks had invited them over for an afternoon swim in the lake.

"Why doesn't somebody cut down all these prickle bushes?" complained Duck.

"They'd just grow back," said Bailey. She stopped and reached into one of the bushes that had scratched her cousin. "Yum," said Bailey, popping a sweet, dark, purple berry into her mouth. "Here, try one."

Duck looked suspicious. "What is it?"

"Blackberry," said Bailey, picking four more. She held them out to him.

Duck looked as if he might like one, but said, "You didn't wash them. Wait, there's a bug." He shoved his hands in his pockets.

Bailey said, "We eat wild berries this way all the time." She blew the little white bug off her hand and continued walking down the path.

"I mean, I like berries," said Duck, hurrying to catch up. "But Grandmother always says we have to wash everything before we eat them."

"Sugar says it's okay to eat wild blackberries the minute we pick them. We're going to make blackberry jam next week."

Duck didn't answer. Bailey easily jumped over the muddy trickle of the creek and deliberately landed in muck. Some splattered on Duck's maroon sneakers. "Now look what happened," he fussed.

"Don't worry about it," said Bailey. "You can rinse them off in the lake and let them dry while we swim."

Dog stopped and sniffed the air. She growled quietly.

"What is it, girl?" said Bailey, petting her. Dog turned her head in the direction of the lake and sniffed harder.

"Do you suppose she smells the bear?" Duck sounded worried. "We shouldn't have come here alone, you know. I need a big stick or something."

"I don't see anything," said Bailey. "Don't worry so much. We're almost there." She didn't sound convincing. She knew what it was like to be a worrier, but Duck seemed to be the king of worriers. She thought about telling Duck to imagine that the bear was small enough to fit in his pocket, but she didn't think he'd like the idea.

Bailey gripped Dog's leash so that she wouldn't follow the wild animal scent into the forest. Dog tugged slightly, then turned and followed Bailey and Duck to the Keswicks' yard.

"Where have you guys been?" yelled Fred. "Everyone's at the waterfront. C'mon." He disappeared down the path to the lake.

"Do we have to go through more woods?" asked Duck. He examined his arms for crawling things.

"It's not far," said Bailey, "and there're more blackberries along the way."

She walked even faster to try to catch up with Fred. "Wait up," said Duck. "Don't leave me alone. There might be snakes. Or a bear."

11

Duck's Fish

When Bailey and Duck reached the lake, Noah was already swimming, and Sparrow was floating on a pink foam noodle. Mr. Will stood next to Sparrow to make sure she didn't drift out too far. Fred tossed his T-shirt on a rock and jumped in, making a huge splash, like the killer whale Bailey had seen at Sea World.

"I'm glad you came," said Mr. Will. "Does your dog like to swim?"

"I don't know," said Bailey. She pulled off the shorts and shirt that covered her neon-green bathing suit and waded in. "Here, girl," she said.

Bailey gently tugged on the leash. Dog followed, then barked as if she wanted Bailey to come out of the water. "It's okay, girl," said Bailey. She tugged again. Dog followed until she was swimming, but she clearly preferred the land. Dog took the leash in her mouth and swam back to shore with it. Bailey laughed. Dog rolled on the shore next to Clover, who was chewing a stick. Then Dog lifted her head and sniffed the air, whined, and sat down.

"What am I supposed to do?" asked Duck. He was still holding his towel and suit.

"Why not go into the boat shed and change," said Mr. Will kindly.

Duck hesitated. Bailey heard him mumble something about spiders and snakes.

When Duck came out of the shed, he rinsed his mud-splattered shoes in the lake and put them on a rock at the edge of the woods behind the shed.

"Can you swim?" asked Mr. Will.

"I took lessons at the YMCA, but I've never been to a lake before. Just a heated pool," said Duck.

"Lake Anna's really warm now," said Mr. Will. "I think you'll like it." He spun Sparrow around, making her squeal.

"What's that?" asked Duck, looking at his feet. The water was up to his knees. "Something touched me."

"It was probably a little fish. A minnow," said Mr. Will.

"A fish?" Duck backed up carefully until he was on the strip of sandy beach. He sat down

45

in a green Adirondack lawn chair and closed his eyes.

"Oh, man," Noah said to Bailey. "What's with your cousin? Is he always like this? I can't believe he's scared of a minnow."

"He hasn't been outside much," said Bailey.

"He's some scaredy dude," said Noah. He splashed her.

Bailey was thinking the same thing.

12

Missing Shoes

"I think we've had enough swimming for one day," said Mr. Will, pushing Sparrow closer to the beach.

"One more time," begged Sparrow. "Just one more." Mr. Will twirled her around in the water again until she shrieked.

Fred, Noah, and Bailey waded into shallow water, letting their suits drip before drying off.

Duck had already changed back into his T-shirt and jeans. His dry bathing suit was rolled back in his towel.

"Where're my shoes?" Duck said. "I left them on the rock near the shed."

"Haven't seen them," said Fred. He put his glasses back on and handed a bottle of water to Sparrow.

"Are you sure it wasn't on a different rock?" asked Noah, towel-drying his hair.

"I know I put them right there." Duck's voice cracked, and he quickly turned his face so no one could see it.

"We'll help you look," said Mr. Will. "Let me get Sparrow ready for the ride up the hill." He put the little girl on top of a picnic table and handed her a yellow towel that was embroidered with the name "Keswick Inn."

The search did not turn up the shoes. "The dogs didn't take them. They were with us all the time," said Fred.

"Sugar just gave me those shoes for wearing in the country," said Duck. His voice trembled.

"I'll bet the boys have an old pair that'll fit you," said Mr. Will. "Now don't worry. You can ride in the tractor wagon with Sparrow on the way back to the house."

Duck walked gingerly across the grassy area, saying, "Ouch ouch," when he stepped on pebbles or sticks. He climbed in the wagon, and Mr. Will placed Sparrow in it with him.

Bailey sighed. She wondered what Sugar would think about Duck's lost shoes. He hadn't even had them a day. The tractor chugged up the hill.

"How long is Duck going to be here?" asked Noah.

"Maybe a couple of weeks," said Bailey. She draped her damp towel around her neck.

"Doesn't he like anything?"

"He likes to invent things," she answered.

"Really!" exclaimed Noah. "Cousin Duck is an inventor. Now that's funny. Fred, we need a list of things to invent at Keswick Inn."

"I'll make a list when we get home, bro," said Fred.

13

Duck's Inventions

Fred gave Duck a pair of tan outgrown sneakers. They fit Duck better than the ones Sugar bought for him at the yard sale.

Miss Bekka handed Duck a small sack with the twins' old T-shirts and shorts for him to use during his visit. He put the bag on a large flat stump near the path to Sugar's house so he wouldn't forget it. Then he returned to the chicken coop, which the neighborhood kids used as a theater and a meeting place.

"Bailey says you invent things, Cousin Duck," said Noah. "Can you invent something for us?"

"Sure," said Duck. "You might have to help build it, though. What do you need invented?"

"I want a machine that washes dishes so I don't have to," said Noah.

"That's called a dishwasher," said Fred. "And we already have one."

"How a about parent-detector so we know when Mom or Dad is coming down the hall?" said Noah.

"That's called Clover. She always barks and runs to greet them," said Fred.

Dog sniffed the air and growled. Bailey said, "It's okay, girl. Just settle down. There's nothing out there."

"Maybe there *is* something out there, like a monster or a bear. How about a monster-detector," said Sparrow, "so we know when it's in the yard?"

"Great idea," said Noah. "Can you invent it, Duck?" Bailey saw Noah wink at Fred.

"Sure," said Duck. "And we'll also make a monster-chaser to frighten monsters away, or maybe a monster-trap."

"Go ahead. Invent. Here's paper," said Fred. He handed Duck his yellow pad.

"I need to think about it," said Duck. "Inventing takes time. You have to consider a lot of things."

"Oh, sure," said Fred, as if he understood. "Whenever you're ready. Just tell us what you need." He smirked at Noah.

"Dad's got a workshop in the barn. He lets us use his tools and things," said Noah. "If we ask."

"A workshop?" Duck suddenly brightened.

"I'm making a shelf for my room there," said Sparrow. "I bent only three nails when I used my hammer."

"Does your dad have pieces of pipe, wire, wood, rope, and scraps of metal?" asked Duck.

"Everything," said Noah. "Dad has everything you need for great inventions, Cousin Duck."

Bailey didn't like the slightly sarcastic tone in the older boy's voice. Even though she wasn't sure that Duck's inventions would work, she didn't think anyone should make fun of him for trying. Fortunately, Duck didn't seem to notice that Noah and Fred were amused by his ideas.

"I'll have a drawing for you tomorrow," said Duck. "Let's go," he said to Bailey.

"Okay," she said.

"Hey, where's my sack of clothes? I know I left it right there." Duck pointed at the stump.

"I didn't see anything," said Noah. "Did you, bro?"

"Nope," said Fred.

"Dog did," said Sparrow. "She was growling about something. I bet it was the bear."

"Bears don't wear clothes," said Fred. "That's silly."

"Can we call your grandmother for a ride?" asked Duck. "I don't feel like walking through the woods."

Bailey had never before asked Sugar to come get her, but with something strange going on in Contrary Woods, she decided it might be a good idea. She picked up Dog's leash and draped it around her neck. Dog yawned and stood up to follow her.

"Hey, hang on," said Duck. He studied the stump. "Look at this."

Fred and Noah were the first to reach him. "Sticks and pebbles," said Duck.

"They're everywhere in the country, Duck," said Noah. "C'mon, let's go."

"Look again," said Duck. "Someone left us a message. Dots and dashes made of stones."

The boys peered over his shoulder.

"Do you think it's a code?" asked Fred.

Duck knelt down for a closer look.

"Maybe it's Morse code?" guessed Bailey. "We learned about it in school, but I don't remember it very well, just how to spell my name."

Duck said, "I know lots of codes. This *is* Morse code. I know all about Samuel Morse and his telegraph system. Look. It's easy. Four dots—the first four stones—are the code for H and the second two stones or dots stand for an I—that spells HI."

"Oh, that's nice. Someone steals your clothes and just says, 'Hi,' " said Noah.

"Who would do that?" asked Bailey.

"At least it's not a bear," said Fred.

"It might be a monster living in the woods," said Sparrow. "Monsters wear clothes." She looked at Bailey and patted her jeans pocket. "I'll put the monster in here," she whispered.

14

Questions

By the time Bailey and Duck returned the next morning, Miss Bekka had rummaged through the family's giveaway clothing bags and found more shorts, shoes, and T-shirts for Duck.

Noah and Fred didn't tell her that the sack had been stolen, nor about the Morse code message. They just let their mother think that somehow the bag had been lost. Miss Bekka was too busy canning garden tomatoes to ask questions.

"If we tell Mom someone stole the clothes, she might get nervous and won't let us hike in the woods without a grown-up," Noah told Bailey and Duck. "We didn't lie. We just said the clothes were, ah, missing."

"Maybe it *would* be good to have a grown-up with us," said Duck. He looked around like he expected to see something scary come crashing from the forest.

"At least the monster is friendly," said Bailey, "and sort of small, or it wouldn't have wanted Duck's clothes."

"I think we should leave a message for your monster," said Fred. "Can you write it, Duck?"

"Sure," said the boy. "What do you want to say?"

"What do you want?" said Fred.

"I don't want anything," said Duck.

"No, Ducky, that's the question to write in code for the monster," said Fred.

"Oh, okay," said Duck. "Help me find small sticks and stones." In just a few seconds he had enough twigs and stones to write "What do you want?"

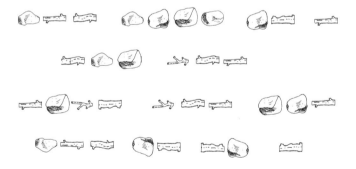

"Do you need a question mark in the code?" asked Bailey.

"Nope," said Duck. "He'll figure out that we're asking a question."

"Wouldn't it be just easier for it to write the message in regular alphabet letters?" asked Fred.

"He knows code, and he can't answer with letters if he doesn't have a pen and paper," said Noah.

"Should we leave something for him?" asked Bailey. "Like a present to show that we're friendly?"

"Like what?" asked Noah.

"I've got a blue feather," said Sparrow. She placed the feather near the message on the stump and put a stone on top of it to keep the wind from blowing it away.

15

Monster Detector

When Bailey and Duck reached the hickory stump the next morning, Duck's code message had been brushed away, the feather was gone, and there was a new message. Duck studied it carefully.

"F-O-O-D," spelled Duck. "It wants food."

"I know that," said Noah, coming up behind them. "Fred and I made a copy of the Morse code last night from a book so we could figure it out, too."

Bailey said, "Do you think we should leave it food? Sugar's got extra canned stuff in the pantry."

"So does Mom," said Fred. "Let's each bring some cans later and see what happens."

"I've got something to show you," said Duck. "Here's my sketch for the monster-detector."

He unfolded a large piece of white paper. Fred took it and Noah looked over his shoulder.

"I'm not sure how it works," said Noah, turning the paper around so he could examine it from all directions.

"First we need to make the box," said Duck, as he pointed out details of the drawing. "Then we add mirrors on these two sides, and a periscope in the center—I know how to make one. Then we hook wires on the back and put the buzzer over here. We put the trip string at this end. Then we connect the whole thing to the wire that goes to your bedroom or the chicken coop, so that you'll know when the monster's around."

"Interesting," said Noah, smiling at Fred.

"I never would have thought of it," said Fred, trying to keep a straight face. "Dad's got most of this stuff in the barn."

Bailey hoped Duck didn't see the twins' expressions.

"And if you want to catch the monster, turn the page over," said Duck. He had drawn detailed directions on how to make a big trap. They would have to dig a hole and cover it with branches. The trap would have an alarm system rigged to the bottom that would make a huge noise. At the same time, a net would fall from a tree and the monster would be trapped and caught.

"Duck, my friend, you're a genius," said Noah. "Let's do both inventions."

Duck put his hands in his pockets and beamed. Then he saw a beetle crawling over his shoe. He jumped up and down and yelled, "Get that thing away from me!"

Bailey saw Noah roll his eyes. She wished Duck weren't so afraid of the outdoors.

16

Justin's Problem

Justin Rudd skidded his rusty bike at the end of the driveway, scattering gravel onto the Keswicks' lawn. His scruffy dog, Ninja, trotted after him. Justin dropped the bike and twisted his orange baseball cap so the bill faced back. He studied Duck.

Bailey couldn't tell what the neighborhood boy thought about her cousin. Justin rarely smiled or joked around, and his brown eyes rarely showed his feelings.

Justin hadn't been nice to her when she arrived. Even though he was nicer now, Bailey knew he didn't like new people—at least he talked that way, when he talked. Most of the time he had little to say around Bailey or the Keswick boys.

Duck's cheeks flushed under the older boy's stare. He turned away and resumed sketching more details of the monster-catcher.

"What's he doin'?" asked Justin.

"Designing a monster-catcher," said Fred. "We're going to build it."

"Ha," said Justin. "No monsters around here. But I heard we've got fur-in-nors coming to town."

"What?" said Mr. Will walking out of the barn with a rake. "What have we got around here, Justin?"

"Fur-in-nors. That's what Ma heard in town."

"Foreigners?"

"Ma heard that they are buying the Dottie-Anna Restaurant—down the Richmond Road—where she works part time."

"Is that a problem?" asked Mr. Will softly. He leaned the rake against the barn.

"Yeah. Ma's worried that she might lose her job if new people buy it." Justin's hands balled into fists.

A wave of concern crossed Mr. Will's face. He ran his fingers through his hair.

Justin looked like he wanted to say something else. He hesitated, as if he were unsure he should repeat more of what his mother had heard. He finally said, "People say the fur-in-nors are different. Kinda brown. And they speak funny."

"I'm brown," said Fred, standing up and taking a step towards Justin. "What's wrong with that?"

"Nothing," mumbled Justin. "There're not brown like you. Besides, it's just what people are saying. Gotta go." He reached down for his bike.

"Wait. I've got work for you, Justin," said Mr. Will. "If you've got the time."

Justin lowered his bike to the ground. "Okay," he said. He stared at Duck again, like the boy was from a distant planet.

As soon as Mr. Will and Justin were out of earshot, Noah said, "Dad'll probably give him one of those talks about being nice to people who're different."

Fred quickly added, "Yeah, like the one he gave us before . . ." He looked away.

Bailey wondered what Fred was about to say. Was it, "before Sparrow arrived with her wheelchair" or, "before they met her cousin Duck"?

Fred didn't finish his sentence. Instead, he said, "Okay, Duck, let's see what you've got."

The younger boy said, "Hang on. I need another minute."

Bailey decided to ask Sugar about the foreigners when she had the opportunity.

17

Bear Returns

"Sorry you missed your grandfather's phone call, Duck," said Sugar. "He said he'd try again later."

"Oh," said Duck. "Okay." Duck looked at his arm. "Yikes!" he said. He dropped his sketches to swat at something. "Go away," he muttered, flicking it to the floor. "Where did it go?" He looked around as if he were under attack.

"Just an ant," said Bailey. She bent down to help him collect his papers.

Duck stomped his feet.

"Your grandmother is doing better," Sugar continued. "She hopes you're having fun, staying clean, and being safe." Sugar waited for Duck's reply.

Duck didn't answer. Instead, he studied the old books that Sugar had purchased at the yard sale. After wiping them off, she had stacked them on the dining room table.

"Help yourself," said Sugar.

Most were hardcover and had lost their dust jackets. Some had a musty odor. Duck wrinkled his nose as he picked up a book with a yellow-green cover.

"Ah, *So Dear to My Heart*—one of my childhood favorites," said Sugar. "About a boy, his strict grandmother, and his pet lamb."

"Interesting," said Duck. He tucked it under his arm.

"I want to read it after you," said Bailey, wishing she had spotted the book first. It sounded good.

Duck nodded and went upstairs with his sketch papers and the book.

Sugar ran her fingers through her short, dyed-brown hair. She said, "Duck doesn't seem to be enjoying his visit very much."

"Not yet," said Bailey. She examined other books in the stacks and picked *Rootabaga Stories* to read before bed.

"A fun book," said Sugar. "Your imagination will work overtime! Good night, dear heart." Bailey gave her grandmother a big hug and went upstairs.

~ ~ ~

In the middle of the night Bailey awoke to the sound of Dog's fierce barking. She dashed down the stairs and bumped into Duck who shouted, "What's going on? I heard a big crash."

Dog was standing on her back legs and snarling at the back door's window.

"What is it, girl?" asked Sugar, petting the dog to calm her down. "It's okay. We're all up now." She turned on the porch light and opened the door. "Nobody's out there."

"Yeah, but look," said Duck, his voice trembling. "The monster has been here. Look at your barbecue."

"Oh, my," said Sugar. The barbecue was flipped on its side. Its top was dented, and the metal grill for cooking was partway across the yard.

"That's no monster. I believe it was Mr. Bear. He must have smelled the bits of burger left on the grill from our dinner last night. I'll see if it can be fixed in the morning," said Sugar. "Let's go back to bed."

"I can't sleep," whined Duck. "Not with that monster bear out there. What if it comes back and breaks a window and comes in and . . ."

"Bailey's dog will protect us," said Sugar firmly. "I'll tell you what. I'll make cocoa, and we'll read together for a while in my study."

She went into the kitchen. Bailey heard her open the refrigerator to get the milk and pop the lid on the cocoa tin. It wouldn't take long to heat the cocoa in the microwave.

"Okay," Duck called after her. "I'm really not afraid, it's just that—" He tried to rub away the goosebumps on his pale arms.

"I know," said Sugar from the kitchen. "Bailey and I aren't afraid, either. We're Wild Women and you can be a Wild Man."

"What do you mean?"

Bailey said, "The Wild Women in the family are brave and adventurous—even when we're scared sometimes."

Sugar returned with mugs of cocoa on a tray and a biscuit for Dog. "Lead the way to my study, and pick a book, Duck," she said.

He looked through the pile of books on the table and pulled out *The Boxcar Children*.

"Another of my favorites," said Sugar.

"Will you read it to us?" asked Duck, curling up on the couch with his mug.

"Sure," said Sugar. "There's a lot of courage in this book."

She began, "One warm night four children stood in front of a bakery. No one knew them. No one knew where they had come from."

By the time she reached the words, "If we don't run away, the baker will take Benny to a Children's Home in the morning," Duck, with a cocoa mustache, was asleep. Dog curled up next to him.

I guess we'll be sleeping in here tonight, thought Bailey.

18

First Invention

"The food's gone," yelled Fred from the edge of the woods.

"Is there another message?" called Bailey. She ran toward the wide stump. Duck tried to keep up. He grumbled about bugs and swatted at small prickly branches that clutched at his clothing.

"Nope," said Noah. "That's weird. You'd think it would have written "T-H-A-N-K-S.""

"Monsters don't always say thank you," said Duck.

"As if you'd know," said Noah.

Bailey wished he didn't have that slightly mean sound to his voice. She hoped Duck didn't notice. If he did, he ignored Noah and walked around the stump, studying the ground.

"We should put it over there," he said, pointing to a cleared area between four pine trees.

"Put what where?" asked Fred.

"The trap. We'll dig a big hole between the trees, put a net at the bottom, tie ropes to the corners, wrap the ropes around the four trees, cover everything with brush and stuff. Then, when the monster falls in, we'll catch him in the net." Duck's pale cheeks reddened with excitement.

Noah rubbed his chin. Bailey waited for him to make a joke, but instead he said, "Okay, pipsqueak, where'll you put the monster-detector?"

"I've been thinking," said Duck. He pointed at a tall hemlock with a fat low branch. "We'll put it on that branch and rig a wire to your bedroom. Then, when the alarm goes off, you can come quickly to pull the ropes, and there you'll have your monster."

He was talking so fast that his words spilled out like cereal pouring into a bowl.

Noah and Fred looked at each other.

"I'll help," said Bailey.

"What'll we tell Mom and Dad if they want to know what we're doing?" asked Fred.

"Just say that we're looking for gold," said Noah. "Let's get the shovels."

Mr. Will and Miss Bekka were gone for the morning. They had taken Sparrow to one of her doctors for a checkup. Noah and Fred carried four shovels out of the barn. "If we hurry, we might get the hole dug before they get back," said Noah.

Bailey tied Dog's leash to a tree and wiped drops of sweat off her forehead. She never dreamed that Virginia would be as hot—maybe even hotter—than Florida was in the summer.

If it were this hot at home, her mother, Molly, would rush into the house after work and say, "Get your stuff, sweetheart. We're going to the beach."

"I'll be ready in a minute," Bailey would answer. She remembered hurrying to her bedroom to change into her bathing suit. Molly would shout from the kitchen, "Looks like we'll have to pick up a picnic somewhere. I guess we ate the last of the cold cuts yesterday."

Bailey knew they would have to get ready quickly because scary thunderstorms with crackling lightning, booming thunder, and heavy rain rolled in almost every afternoon. Then the sky would turn as black as licorice, and the rain and wind would be so strong that there was no point wearing a raincoat or carrying an umbrella.

If the storm arrived when they drove into the beach parking lot, they would sit in the car, listening to Molly's favorite CDs until the pelting rain stopped. The hard rain always wiped the beach clean of the day's footprints. Then Bailey and Molly's feet would make new prints as they raced across the sand to the shining water to watch the sunset.

Footprints. Without much summer rain, the Virginia red soil was hard-packed except for mushy puddles near the creeks. The soil didn't welcome footprints. It didn't welcome shovels, either.

"Dang," said Fred. "This is terrible." He stopped digging and leaned on his shovel. "This is going to take us till we're one hundred years old."

"I give up," said Noah. "We've been working for an hour and have dug down only a couple of inches."

Fred said, "So, what's next, Mr. Inventor?"

Duck looked unconcerned. "I'll figure out something."

19

Justin Explodes

Duck was squatting under the apple tree sketching a new monster trap when Justin rode up. He skidded his bike, deliberately spraying pebbles at Duck. The young boy looked up in alarm, but kept his mouth shut.

Bailey knew she should say something, especially since Justin had not been friendly to anyone lately. He had been scowling and glaring ever since he had told them about the "fur-in-nors" who might be buying the place where his mother worked. That didn't give him the right to pick on Duck.

"Hey," yelled Bailey. She was about to add, "That wasn't nice," but Justin dropped his bike and walked quickly toward the barn to look for Mr. Will. Ninja panted behind him.

"Are you okay?" Bailey asked Duck.

"Yeah," he said, brushing the dirt and stones off his lap. "I'd like to catch that jerk in my trap," he added, going back to his design. Bailey wanted to see Duck's latest sketch, but he tipped his paper to keep her from peeking.

Suddenly, they heard yelling in the barn, crashing noises, and more yelling.

Justin dashed out. Blood trickled from his nose, and his face was a mask of fiery anger. He jumped on his bike and tore away. Ninja sped to catch up.

Bailey and Duck ran to the barn. While her eyes adjusted to the dark, she heard Mr. Will say, "Are you all right, Son?" He bent over Noah, who was rubbing his face.

"Ouch. Ouch," said Noah. "Don't touch it."

"Can you stand up?" asked Mr. Will.

"I'm okay," said Noah, getting to his feet.

"What happened?" asked his father.

"Nothing," mumbled Noah, trying to get away.

"Don't tell me that. Justin dashed past me with a bloody nose, and you're getting quite a shiner."

Mr. Will lifted Noah's chin so they were looking at each other. "You know I don't believe in settling things with fists. Stand up for yourself, but talk it out."

Noah's lips pursed stubbornly. He didn't speak.

"I mean it, Son. Now, I think you should put an ice pack on that eye," said Mr. Will, studying Noah's face. Redness surrounded his left eye.

"Duck, could you go to the house and ask Miss Bekka for a bag of ice?"

"Sure, Mr. Will." Duck sounded pleased to be useful.

"Now, Son, I need to know what happened. Justin has been a good helper around here, and his family needs money. We've got to get things straightened out, and that starts with you." Mr. Will's voice was calm but firm.

Noah sat on a bale of hay and looked at barn swallows swooping in the rafters. "It's about his mom. Justin was going to tell you that he thinks she'll lose her job because the foreigners *did* buy the Dottie-Anna Restaurant. Her friend, Cookie, the cook, is already gone."

Mr. Will looked worried. "So, what was the fight about?"

Noah hesitated, then muttered, "I said that maybe if his mom was a better waitress, the new people would keep her. And he punched me, and I slugged him back. It was stupid, and I didn't even mean it when I said it."

Mr. Will's brows furrowed. "Yes, that was an unfortunate and hurtful thing to say. Mrs.

Rudd is an excellent waitress and works hard to support her family. I want you to apologize. We're going over there right now."

"I know," said Noah.

"I will also speak to Justin about fighting, but you must take responsibility for your own words and actions. Words can hurt even more than a black eye or a bloody nose, Noah. That kind of hurt can last longer than bruises."

"I'm sorry, Dad," said Noah. He stood up and followed Mr. Will to their van. Duck handed him the ice and he put it on his face when he climbed inside.

No wonder Justin was so upset, thought Bailey. *I would have been, too.*

20

Goldie

Shortly after Bailey turned out the light, Dog climbed on the bed and stretched out next to her. Dog sighed. Bailey rolled over so she could wrap her arms around her and rub her soft spotted belly. Bailey was pleased that Shadow and Sallie no longer ran away when Dog settled next to Bailey. They arranged themselves around Bailey's head, purring quietly.

Bailey felt bad that she hadn't come up with a good name for her friend yet. Fred's list of names was longer and longer. Even her mother and Norma Jean had added their ideas in their e-mails. Molly suggested "Bess," after one of the Wild Women, and Norma Jean thought "Fang" would be funny.

Angel isn't such a bad name, thought Bailey. *How about Angel Fish?* She smiled. She looked out the dormer window at the night sky. *Star. Star Fish.* She smiled again. *Maybe Star*

Angel Fish. Angel could be Dog's middle name.
Dog could have lots of names, like Duck.

Bailey remembered a time when she and her Mom spent a weekend with friends on Sanibel Island, about an hour from their Port Charlotte home. Whenever they visited these friends, Molly would wake Bailey early so they could walk on the beach and see the bright orange-and-pink sunrise. Sometimes they

waded into the Gulf of Mexico and got their PJs wet. One morning, Bailey saw her first starfish swimming near shore. It had the same brown colors as Dog.

While Bailey looked for shells, Molly sipped coffee from a travel mug and squinted at the laughing gulls and pelicans hunting for food while they glided low over the silvery water. More than once, Bailey saw a faraway look in her mom's eyes.

"It would be wonderful to fly away," Molly had said. "To see what's on the other side of the Gulf—Mexico and beyond, even to Central and South America. To see the Pacific Ocean. To have adventures, don't you think, girl-friend?"

Bailey hadn't answered. When her mom talked about having faraway adventures, Bailey felt uneasy, like when she worried that she might get lost in a store. To change the subject, Bailey quickly held out shells for Molly to identify.

"Let's see," said her mom, "you found a lim-pet, a scallop, a goldie—that's my own name for jingle shells because many are gold—co-quinas, a fighting conch, and that one's a cat's paw." Bailey studied the little shells. The goldie was shiny orange.

"Turn it over, and you'll see what looks like a baby's footprint inside. Sometimes you'll find black ones or other colors, but I like the or-ange ones the best. My friends and I used to string goldies with holes into necklaces."

Bailey's goldie didn't have a hole. She put the shells in her beach jacket pocket.

"Shell collectors aren't interested in them, but these ordinary shells are beautiful in their own way, aren't they?" said her mother. "It's important to look for what's beautiful in the ordinary. They're all special, but the goldie's my favorite."

Molly tousled Bailey's hair and said, "Race you." Off they ran on the hard-packed sand that was filled with new shells that had washed in on the morning high tide.

Goldie.

Suddenly Bailey knew what she wanted to name her dog with the orange spot on her neck. Goldie. Dog had come from Ordinary Road, but she was special. And when they moved back to Florida, Bailey would take Goldie with her for a run on the beach when the orange sun was rising.

"At last you have a name," she said softly, stroking Goldie's ears. "And your middle names will be Star and Angel."

Goldie whined in her sleep. Her paws twitched like she was having a dream about running.

21

Mystery in Contrary Woods

"C'mon, Goldie," coaxed Bailey. The dog wagged her tail, but didn't get off the bed. Bailey was dressed in a red T-shirt and shorts made from cutoff jeans. "C'mon, girl, we've got to tell everyone your true name."

Goldie dropped to the floor with a thud and ambled toward the door. Shadow perched on the window ledge in the dormer.

"What is it, kitten?" asked Bailey. Shadow purred when she stroked his gray back. Bailey looked outside and saw Sugar shaking her head and picking up the birdbath's stand and basin. They had been toppled during the night and needed to be reassembled.

"Uh-oh, the bear must have been back," said Bailey.

By the time she reached the kitchen, her grandmother was coming up the porch steps with a broken feeder.

"We had a visitor again. Take a look at the giant paw prints on the porch," said Sugar. "I can forgive him for knocking over the birdbath, but he tore up another young apple tree. Now, that wasn't nice at all especially when he could have had lovely big apples this fall. And something else—either the bear or a deer—ate our little watermelon." Sugar put her hands on her hips, then smiled.

Bailey wondered if Duck would be even more afraid if he saw how big the bear's paws were. "I heard Goldie growl a lot," said Bailey, "but I didn't know it was at the bear."

"Who's Goldie?" asked Duck, yawning. Bailey hadn't heard him come into the kitchen.

"That's Dog's new name," Bailey said. "I just thought of it. The bear actually came on the porch last night. I'll show you its footprints." Duck's eyes grew wide with alarm.

"Nice name," said Sugar. "That's what Molly called the jingle shells—the shells she gave to her best friends when she was your age."

"I know," said Bailey, with a grin. She filled Goldie's bowl with kibble and put two dishes of cat food on the washing machine so Goldie couldn't steal Shadow and Sallie's food.

Bailey thought Duck might want to know all the reasons she'd come up with that name for her dog, but as usual, he didn't seem even a little curious. Instead, her cousin helped himself to toast and blackberry jam. He examined the jam suspiciously.

"What are you up to today?" asked Sugar. She poured herself another cup of coffee and opened the morning paper.

"Going over to the Keswicks'," said Bailey.

"What's happening there these days?" Sugar slowly turned the pages in the front section.

Bailey and Duck exchanged glances. He shook his head and put his finger to his lips.

"Just stuff," she said. "Doing things."

"If I'm not here when you come home for lunch, help yourself to chicken salad and blackberry pie," said Sugar.

"Okay," said Duck. He put his plate in the sink and turned to leave the room. Without looking up, Sugar cleared her throat. Duck returned to the sink, washed his plate, and put it in the drainer.

"Thanks," said Sugar. She was still engrossed in reading the newspaper.

"I'll be ready in a minute," said Duck.

"I'd keep Goldie on a leash again today," said Sugar. "I heard hounds in the woods last night. She might want to chase after them."

"Why?" asked Bailey. "This is her home now." She rubbed Goldie's back.

"Sometimes abandoned hunting dogs want to return to the pack," said Sugar. "It was how they were raised—to run together."

"I'll hang onto her," said Bailey.

"Ready," said Duck. He looked like a country kid in his "new" clothes. He tucked his pad of invention ideas under his arm.

Bailey snapped Goldie's leash to her collar. "Race you," she said to Duck.

When they reached the big hickory stump, they found Fred and Noah decoding the latest message with their Morse code sheet. "It's just like text messaging," said Noah. "The thing writes us, and we write him. Let's see what it wants now."

"M-O-R-E F-O-O-D," read the dots and dashes fashioned from sticks and stones.

"If we take more food out of the pantry, Mom's gonna know," said Fred. "We can't keep giving it away like that."

"Well, I want to know what's going on," said Noah. The area around his eye was blue and yellow, but the swelling had gone down. "I'm going into the woods to find out."

"I heard your mother say do not go in there because of the bear," said Duck.

"You don't have to go with me, squirt," said Noah. "Who's coming?"

"I'm in," said Fred.

"Me, too," said Bailey. She was a little scared, but didn't want to be left behind when the boys were off on an adventure.

Duck said nothing. His face was pale and worried. Bailey said, "Why don't you see what Sparrow's doing? I bet she'd like company."

Duck looked relieved. "Okay," he said.

"Just don't tell," said Fred.

"You can't bring Dog with you," Noah said to Bailey. "She might bark or make noise. We've got to be really quiet or whatever it is will know that we're coming."

"I named my dog Goldie," said Bailey. She had hoped that the boys would ask about her dog's new name, but all they could think about was searching for the mysterious person or monster in the woods. "Where should I put her?"

"The Chicken Coop Theater," said Noah. "She'll be okay in there for a little while."

"I guess so," said Bailey. "C'mon, girl."

Goldie trotted alongside Bailey until they reached the fixed-up chicken coop. "I'll be back soon. Be good, Goldie," said Bailey. Her dog tried to follow her but Bailey quickly shut the door. She could hear Goldie barking, whining, and scratching. "No noise," Bailey said. She jogged back to where the boys were waiting.

"We've got to be very quiet," said Noah. "Watch your every step. We don't want the Morse code person to know we're coming. Now, follow me."

Noah took slow steps to avoid kicking a stone or snapping a fallen stick. He carefully pushed branches out of his way without letting them crack. Fred and Bailey moved cautiously behind him, stepping where Noah stepped. Goldie's barking became fainter as they crept deeper into the woods. After a few minutes, they came to a hard-packed dirt road with ruts.

"How do you know we're going the right way?" asked Fred quietly. His face was sweaty. He took off his glasses and wiped them on his T-shirt.

"A hunch," Noah whispered. "Whoever makes the messages has to be far enough away from Sugar's property and our path to the lake so we can't easily see him, but close enough to find us. Dad told me when we moved here that there used to be an old cabin where people lived who worked in the mines along Contrary Creek. I want to look there first."

He crossed the road and ducked into the thick woods. Bailey and Fred followed. She wished she had brought Goldie along for protection.

22

Strangers

"Freeze," hissed Noah. "Don't make a sound."

Bailey tried to peer over his shoulder, but Noah was too tall. "I can't see," she whispered back.

"Will you look at that!" Noah said in amazement.

"What?" said Fred. "Hunker down so we can see."

Noah bent over. Bailey's eyes opened wide. In a small hilly clearing about fifty feet ahead of them was an old brown station wagon. To its right was a clothesline tied between oak trees. The line was draped with pants and shirts of various sizes and a pair of maroon sneakers. An olive green army blanket was stretched like a tent roof between the car's doors to create shade.

To the left of the station wagon, someone had made a fire pit and surrounded it with rocks. Six plastic gallon water jugs were lined up in a row near the front tire.

"What are you doing? Spying on us?" said a sharp voice behind them. Bailey was so startled that she grabbed Fred's arm.

Noah stood up, whirled around, and said, "We're not spying, ma'am."

"Sure looks like it to me," the woman said. Her brown hair was cropped short like a boy's, and she wore a smudged gray tank top and khaki shorts. She was taller than Miss Bekka, and thin. Her arms and legs were covered with scratches and bug bites. The woman put her hands on her hips and glared at them. "You're creeping up on us and hiding. I certainly call that spying."

"These are our woods," said Noah. His voice cracked slightly. "My parents own them. All the way to the lake."

"Don't be so sure of that, kid. And even if they do, they don't need this little corner. We do." There were daggers in her voice. "We're not bothering anyone."

Bailey looked back at the station wagon and saw two small children and a boy about her age peering from behind it.

"Now go away and leave us alone. And don't come back," the woman said. She stepped protectively between Bailey, Noah, and Fred and the old station wagon.

Bailey looked again at the sneakers and T-shirts hanging on the line. They seemed familiar.

The woman was still scowling. "Go away. Vamoose. Get lost," she said.

"Okay," said Fred. "We're going." He stood up and stumbled over a bush. Noah followed him. Bailey looked back at the station wagon again. There was no sign of the children.

"We could bring you food and stuff," Bailey called to the woman.

"We don't need anything from anyone," said the woman. "Now get out of here!" Her voice was as hostile as a disturbed hornets' nest.

Bailey, Fred, and Noah walked quickly toward the dirt road, not now caring if they made noise.

When they were well beyond the road, Bailey said, "Those people must be living in the woods. I bet one of the kids has been telling us they need food. Did you see the clothes on the line that looked like the ones that were stolen from Duck?"

"You might be right," said Noah. "What a nasty woman! What gives her the right to camp her crummy station wagon there?"

"It's time to tell Mom and Dad. They'll know what to do," said Fred.

"Sugar can help, too," said Bailey.

"Not yet," said Noah. "I want to get proof that they are the ones leaving messages and stealing from us."

"How are you going to do that?" asked Fred.

"Duck," said Noah.

23

Invisible

Duck listened carefully when Noah breathlessly told him that he needed to invent a different monster-catcher—one that didn't need a hole because it was too hard to dig one.

"How big do you want the trap?" asked Duck. "I mean, how big is the monster?"

"It's not terribly big," said Noah. "Maybe my size."

"Sure," said Duck. "That's easy. I've been thinking that it would be cool to use a dog to help scare the monster into the trap. We could use Bailey's dog, Gilda."

"Goldie, not Gilda," said Bailey. "I already told you that." Nobody was listening. "Am I invisible?" she asked her dog. Goldie thumped her tail.

Duck added, "If we tied Gilly to the tree near the trap, with a really long leash, she'd bark and . . ."

"Her name isn't Gilly, it's Gilda, I mean Goldie," said Bailey. "Now, you're making me confused."

The boys didn't answer. Fred squatted next to Duck, and Noah bent down to watch. He said, "Just start drawing, Cousin Duck." Noah reached out and rubbed Goldie's head.

"I thought you'd want to hear what I'm calling my dog," said Bailey loudly.

"I think Jelly is a cool name for her," said Noah. "Really." He gazed intently at Duck's drawing. "Hey, that's really awesome. I think the dog is what'll make it work."

"Thanks," said Duck.

I am invisible, thought Bailey. *I might as well go home. And they can find someone else's dog to scare the monster into the trap!*

24

Explorers and Inventors

"I need to go to Charlottesville tomorrow," said Sugar when supper was served. "We'll make a day of it."

Bailey and Duck looked at each other. They had planned to return to Keswick Inn to work on his inventions. Duck twirled his fork over his mashed potatoes.

"What's in Charlottesville?" he asked. "I mean, can't we stay at the Keswicks' tomorrow while you go?"

"It's a good day for us to do some exploring together," Sugar said. "Just the three of us."

Duck smoothed his potatoes into what looked to Bailey like the big tree stump. He made a few dots and dashes on the top. "I like reading about explorers and inventors," he said, "but hasn't everything been explored?"

Sugar glanced at Duck's mashed potatoes, then said, "Bailey and I like to explore new places by taking rides on roads we don't know. The Charlottesville area is particularly lovely because you can see the mountains. President Thomas Jefferson lived near there at Monticello. We'll take a tour of his magnificent house and grounds tomorrow."

Duck looked like he might take a bite of potatoes, then put his fork down.

"Besides being a president, Jefferson was an admirer of designs and gadgets," Sugar added. "He actually invented three things—a special sundial, a type of plow, and a cipher wheel for coding and decoding messages . . ."

Duck interrupted. "We studied about him. My teacher said that Jefferson liked learning about other people's inventions, like the macaroni extruder."

"A macaroni what?" asked Bailey.

"You know, a pasta machine. The extruder squeezes the dough into the shape of noodles," said Duck. He stirred gravy into the potatoes changing the tree stump into white mushy mountains with a brown gravy river.

"And Jefferson was also interested in exploration," said Sugar.

Duck studied his plate.

"Lewis and Clark," she continued. "They were from the Charlottesville area."

"Oh, yeah," said Duck. "I know about them."

"Clark was one of my ancestors," said Bailey. "Sugar showed me his name in the family tree."

Duck draped a thick piece of steak across the river to make a bridge and balanced three peas. They looked like little green people. "I wish I had an explorer in the family."

Bailey looked at Sugar, then said, "Well, maybe because you are my sort-of cousin, Clark can be your sort-of ancestor, too."

Duck smiled the best smile Bailey had seen since he had arrived. He scooped up the first potato mountain with his fork and ate it in one gulp.

"Sounds cool, but I don't want to go with you tomorrow. I want to hang out with Noah and Fred. We've got things to do. Hope you don't mind." He took his plate to the sink and quickly washed it.

Bailey *did* mind. It wasn't that Duck was tons of fun to be around, but she felt more invisible than ever because he wanted to go to Keswick Inn without her. And why were the twins—*her* friends—suddenly more interested in Duck than in her? Bailey tried to hide her disappointment from Sugar, who was trying to plan special activities during Duck's visit.

"It'll be great to go to Charlottesville, Sugar," said Bailey. "Just you and me."

"You bet. We'll have a grand time," said Sugar. "Just the Wild Women."

"Sure," said Bailey.

25

More E-Mail

It was Bailey's turn to use the computer first after she and Duck finished cleaning the kitchen. He said, "Fifteen minutes. That's all you get," which annoyed Bailey. *This is my house and my grandmother's computer,* she thought. *I'll take longer if I want to.*

From: Mollyf2@travl.net
To: "Bailey"<baileyfish@gmail.com>
Sent: 8 p.m.
Subject: the dog

I think it's great Sugar has gotten a dog to keep her company. We always had dogs when I was growing up. Poor Andrew is so allergic to animals that if I even mention a dog or cat he sneezes. It's a good thing he studies bugs, not something with fur. How are things going with Cousin Duck? I remember Uncle Max--that's what I always called him. We sometimes visited with him and Duck's father when I was a kid. Duck's father was a bit younger. He liked to make things.

I have to get back to work. Andrew wants to review the draft of my next chapter about him tonight, and then we'll send it to the publisher.
xxxooo Mom

What on earth was Mom talking about? Why did it matter if Dr. Andrew Snorge-Swinson was allergic to dogs—Goldie or any other one? Bailey already knew that Bug Man sneezed around cats. He made her keep Shadow and Sallie outside when he came to Sugar's house on his way to New York City with Bailey's mom. She wanted to ask her mom about what happened to Duck's father, but at the moment Bailey was more concerned about Dr. Snorge-Swinson and dogs.

From:"Bailey"baileyfish@gmail.com>
To: Mollyf2@travl.net
Sent: 6:45 p.m.
Subject: reply

Hey, Mom: I named her Goldie, and she's really wonderful. She's gentle and friendly and protects us. She doesn't chew the furniture or chase the cats. Her coat's very soft and silky. I know you'll like her. She's not really Sugar's dog. She's MINE. Here's a picture of her. I think the white on her face looks like a bone.

When we go back to Florida, Goldie can sleep on my bed like she does here. She'll guard you, too. Love, Bailey

Bailey attached the picture to the e-mail message, just like Sugar showed her how to do.

My dog Goldie.jpg

"Aren't you done yet?" Duck complained from the doorway to Sugar's office.

"Nope," said Bailey. "Soon." She didn't care if he was annoyed with her.

26

Muffins at the Dottie-Anna

Duck barely muttered thanks when Sugar dropped him off at Keswick Inn the next morning. He shoved the car door open with his foot, grabbed his sketch pad, and ran toward the inn's porch were the boys were waiting. Duck was in such a hurry that he didn't close the truck door all the way, and Bailey had to reach over to do it. She slammed the door extra hard.

"Ouch," said Sugar, looking at Bailey. "Your face tells me that you aren't happy about something this morning. Want to talk?"

Bailey shook her head and twisted her hair behind her ears.

"I'm a pretty good listener," said Sugar, pushing her glasses up higher on her nose.

Bailey actually had a lot she wanted to talk about. She stared out the window as the truck crossed Contrary Creek. Where would she begin? Should she ask about the foreigners, or tell Sugar about the message stump, or the woman in the woods, or what a pain Duck could be? Should she tell Sugar about her mother's e-mail about Bug Man and his allergy to dogs as well as cats?

When Bailey didn't answer immediately, Sugar turned on the radio—her favorite classical station—and hummed along to a Mozart symphony. Every once in a while, Bailey saw Sugar looking at her with a crinkly smile. Bailey finally smiled back and hummed with her until they both laughed.

"Hey, this isn't the way to Charlottesville," said Bailey.

"No, I thought we'd stop by the Dottie-Anna for homemade muffins—a little treat."

"That's where Mrs. Rudd works," said Bailey, "unless she's been fired." The words just slipped out.

"Fired? Why would that happen?" asked her grandmother.

"Justin says that foreigners bought the restaurant, and his mother might lose her job."

"Hmmm," said Sugar. "I don't know why he would think that."

The red pickup pulled into the little restaurant's gravel parking lot. Bailey didn't see Mrs. Rudd's car. She hopped out of the truck and followed Sugar into the Dottie-Anna. Gone were the drab-green plaid café curtains and the nicked wooden tables. Fresh yellow and white stripped curtains hung in the windows, and the walls were painted light blue. The place no longer smelled like dirty ashtrays. NO-SMOKING signs were prominently displayed. The floor had been scrubbed, and the burned-out light bulbs had been replaced.

"Looks and smells much better," said Sugar. "Where do you want to sit?" Bailey pointed to the counter. She liked the round swivel stools with shiny yellow vinyl seats.

The new owner, wearing a name tag that read MELE, wiped the counter and asked if they were ready to order. Sugar said, "Black coffee, please," and pointed to a carrot muffin under a glass dome. Bailey said, "I'll have orange juice and one of those." The woman lifted the lid on a clear plastic case and slid a chocolate-covered donut onto a white china plate.

Bailey studied her. She was kind of like Justin described. Light brown skin, dark brown eyes and hair, and she wore a colorful scarf draped around her neck. She spoke English very clearly, but she did have a teeny accent.

"You've done a nice job fixing up this place," said Sugar.

"Thank you," said the woman.

"One of our neighbors works here, but I don't see her today," Sugar continued. "Nora. Nora Rudd."

"Oh, yes, Nora," said the woman. "She's a good worker when she comes, but I worry about her. She's been calling in sick lately. I fear she doesn't like having a new boss." The woman wiped the shiny white counter and carried dirty mugs to the sink. "I must have helpers that I can count on."

"Nora's a good woman," Sugar said. "I'm sure there's an explanation." She stirred her coffee thoughtfully.

"I hope so," said the new owner. "Please excuse me." She picked up the pot of coffee and went over to a table by the window where other customers were finishing their french toast with whipped cream and strawberries.

Yummy. I'll order that the next time, thought Bailey.

27

Finding the Way

"So what are you going to do about Mrs. Rudd?" asked Bailey when they got back to the pickup.

"We'll stop by to see her—to find out what's going on," said her grandmother. "Now, get out the Virginia map and tell me which way is the best to go from here to Monticello."

"Don't you know? You've lived here a long time."

"I have my ideas," said Sugar, "but I'd like to hear what you think."

Bailey opened the map and traced the routes from Sugar's house down the Richmond Road. "Is this where we are?" she asked.

Her grandmother leaned over to have a look. "Pretty close."

Bailey said, "I can't find Monticello."

"Look near Charlottesville," said Sugar.

Bailey studied the map carefully. "Oh, here it is. We could take Route 64, or the little roads."

"Which do you prefer?" asked Sugar. "We'll see the mountains either way."

"Let's take 64 over and the little roads coming back," said Bailey. "We can see different sights then."

"Spoken like an adventurous Wild Woman," said Sugar. She turned the key in the ignition, and off they headed to Charlottesville on the four-lane highway.

Bailey wondered what Duck and the Keswicks were doing. Had they decided on a design for the trap? Would they be building it without her? Were they keeping it a secret from Sparrow so she wouldn't tell anyone?

And what about the woman in the woods with the kids? When Bailey and her mom lived in Florida there were lots of homeless people—many of them were women and children. Some of them lived in camps in the woods. She and her mom bought canned goods at the store to donate to the food pantry. This women said she didn't want food, but someone had left a message on the stump asking for something to eat. Noah wanted to set a trap, but was that the right thing to do?

Bailey was going to tell Sugar about the woman when her grandmother said, "I think the two of us need to practice the piano more this summer. I think it would be fun to have a musical party before school starts again."

"I'm still not very good," said Bailey.

"Me, neither," said Sugar with a laugh, "but we could have a lot of fun. And you can play your clarinet at the party, too."

"Fred plays guitar, and Noah has bongo drums," said Bailey.

"I've been saving jugs," said Sugar. "Maybe the other guests could be in a jug band."

"What's a jug band?" Bailey was puzzled.

"You fill the empty jugs with varying amounts of water, and they make different notes when you blow across the top. Everyone plays their note in turn."

"That sounds like fun," said Bailey. She already liked the idea.

"It's fun to do silly things sometimes," said her grandmother. "Hey, navigator, isn't this our turn?" asked Sugar.

"Oops. Yes," said Bailey.

28

A Curious Mind

Peas. Bailey nudged Sugar a second time. Her grandmother was listening intently to their guide tell them about the two meals a day served at Monticello. Bailey noticed in the dining room that one of the displays included a bowl of peas, the president's favorite vegetable. She wanted Sugar to see it.

Sugar smiled, but held her finger to her lips. They would talk about the house later, after the tour was over.

Bailey was amazed by the inventions and objects that interested Thomas Jefferson. The tour had started in the entrance hall, then continued through a sitting room, a book room or library, past a green house, his study, his bedroom, a parlor, and then entered the dining room. Bailey had been intrigued by a copying machine called a "polygraph" on one of the desks. Thomas Jefferson hadn't invented it, but he liked using it because when he wrote with one pen connected to another, his writing was duplicated.

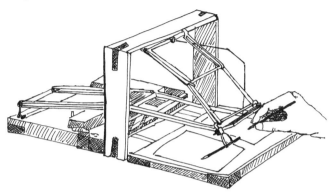

Hawkins and Peale polygraph—an early copying machine displayed on Jefferson's desk in his study.

In the first few rooms Bailey had seen inventions and scientific equipment. She learned that he often made improvements to inventions that he saw or owned. In his house were microscopes, unusual clocks, a machine to measure the wind speed and direction, telescopes, and compasses, a book stand to hold five open books, and a dumbwaiter, like a little elevator that went between floors.

Wherever Bailey looked, she could see that this tall, redheaded president was curious about everything. He was curious about science, Native-Americans, animals, plants, and farming methods. He learned much from the books in his large collection. Even though most of his 6,700 books had been sold to the Library of Congress, fifty of his leather-bound books had been found and were now carefully preserved in a special glass case at Monticello. Bailey knew her grandmother wanted to stay in the library area longer, but the tour had continued through the downstairs.

"Now we can talk," said Sugar, when they were back outside. "Are your feet pooped, or shall we wander down to where this wonderful president is buried. We'll stop at the gift shop on the way back."

"Let's wander," said Bailey.

They walked past Mulberry Row, the site of former plantation workshops and a few slave cabins. Below Mulberry Row, they saw square gardens filled with vegetables and flowers. At the bottom of a steep brick walk was the Jefferson family cemetery.

"So, what did you like the best about our visit?" asked Sugar, when they boarded the shuttle bus to return to their pickup.

"I liked it all," said Bailey. "Duck should have come."

"You'll have to tell him about our day," said Sugar.

If Duck's curious, thought Bailey.

29

Reassuring Mrs. Rudd

"Let's stop at the Rudds' before we pick up Duck," said Sugar. "I'd like to check on Nora."

Bailey knew that times had been hard for the Rudd family ever since Mr. Rudd was arrested for deliberately polluting Contrary Creek. Then to make matters worse, he broke out of jail while he was waiting for his trial and came to Sugar's house. He smashed her window and threatened her to try to keep her from testifying against him. Bailey shuddered. He was a scary man, and mean to Justin and his sisters.

Nora answered the door on the second ring. Bailey didn't see Fern or any of Justin's other little sisters. Maybe they were watching him carve things in his special workshop or helping him feed his pet crow, Chuck.

Mrs. Rudd's eyes were puffy and red.

Sugar said nothing but gave her a long hug.

"Come in," said Mrs. Rudd. "It's too hot to sit on the porch at this hour in the afternoon sun."

"I stopped by the Dottie-Anna today," said Sugar. She waited for Mrs. Rudd to respond, but she didn't.

"They miss you at work," Sugar continued.

"I haven't felt well," Mrs. Rudd finally said.

"Oh," said Sugar. "Have you been to the doctor?"

"It's not that," said Mrs. Rudd. Her voice trailed off.

Sugar sat down on the couch. Bailey wasn't sure she should stay in the room, but no one told her to leave so grown-ups could talk in private. She wandered over to the side window and looked out.

"I see there are new owners," said Sugar.

"Yes," said Mrs. Rudd. "The Kamakas. Mele and Alika."

"Mele seems nice. I haven't met her husband yet." Sugar's statement seemed more like a question.

"Oh, yes," said Nora. "It's just that I'm afraid."

"Afraid of what, Nora?"

"What if I lose my job? What if someone tells them about Ruby being in jail? I haven't felt well."

Ruby? Bailey had never heard Mr. Rudd's first name before.

"None of that should make a difference if you go to work and do a good job. Every family has problems and difficult family members. Hold your head up and give the new owners a chance to get to know you."

After a moment, Mrs. Rudd sighed and said, "I'll try. Will you have some iced tea?"

"Not today, thanks. We've got to pick up Duck and get supper on the table."

Before Bailey turned to follow her grandmother to the door, she saw Justin in the field beyond his workshop. He raised his arm over his head and hurled one rock and then another at a small oak tree.

30

S-O-R-R-Y

Duck had little to say during supper. He arranged his asparagus stalks into a log-cabin design before eating them.

Bailey thought he would want to know what they saw at Monticello. When he asked no questions about their day, she volunteered, "Did you know that Thomas Jefferson made his own version of vanilla ice cream? We saw a picture of his handwritten recipe."

"Uh-huh," said Duck, studying his pork chop as if he wanted to make it into something different, like a boat. "I learned all about him in school," he said.

Sometimes Duck was such a snotty know-it-all that Bailey felt like finding a caterpillar to put in his shoe. She slipped a piece of meat to Goldie, who was waiting patiently next to her chair.

"What did you do today?" Sugar asked the boy.

"Stuff," said Duck. "Neat stuff. Guy stuff."

Bailey winced. Guy stuff. This didn't sound good at all. She wished that Duck's grandfather would come back for him soon so that Noah and Fred would want to do things with her again. She imagined putting a caterpillar in each of Duck's shoes.

"Let's play dominoes after you're done with the dishes. I think the set's in the attic," said Sugar. "Be back in a minute." She pushed her chair away from the table.

"Well, I'm going back to Keswicks' tomorrow," said Bailey firmly. "You wash, I'll dry." She tossed a sponge at Duck and got a fresh towel out of a drawer.

He frowned. "Don't wreck things," he said under his breath.

"What do you mean?" asked Bailey.

"You can't tell." He handed her a rinsed plate. "You know, about the people, the monster, and the trap."

"Were there more code messages?" asked Bailey.

"Yes," said Duck. "The first one said, 'Don't follow me.' Then, when we looked later, there was another. It spelled, 'S-O-R-R-Y.' "

"Why was it sorry?" asked Bailey. She opened the cupboard and carefully stacked the plates.

"Maybe it was sorry that it stole Miss Bekka's pie that she left on the porch table to cool. Or maybe it was sorry that it took her favorite blue T-shirt off the line. Noah says he'll make the monster sorry all right when he catches him with our trap."

Bailey was relieved that Duck was talking to her again.

"Did you finish designing the trap yet?" she asked, wiping and rewiping a glass until it sparkled.

"Almost. It'll just take another hour or so, then we can start building it. I know it'll work. Quiet. Here she comes."

"Found them," said Sugar. "The dominoes were in my closet, however, not the attic. Pull up your chairs."

"But I wanted to use the computer," said Duck. "It's my turn to go first."

"Not tonight," said Sugar. "I've declared this game night. Now, here's how we play chicken foot dominoes."

She dumped black cubes with white dots on the kitchen table.

31

W-A-T-C-H

The bear returned to the Keswicks' that night and tried to get in the barn window where the bird feeders were stored. Mr. Will showed everyone claw marks on the wooden siding.

"Maybe it wasn't a bear, but a monster," said Duck. "It doesn't really matter because we'll find out when the trap's set."

"I want you to invent a flying machine for me," said Sparrow, "so I don't have to roll around in this chair anymore."

"Maybe, when I'm done with the trap," Duck said. He took out his pencil and scribbled something on his pad.

"How about a musical instrument?" asked Bailey. "You could invent something to bring to the music party that Sugar's going to have soon."

"I'll think about it," said Duck. "Here." He handed his sketches of the monster-detector and trap to Noah. Fred whistled. "Way cool. Let's get started," he said.

"Bailey, you and Sparrow wait here. Let us know if anyone is coming. Let's go, guys," Noah said. He and the boys went inside the barn to look for supplies. Clover scampered in circles around them.

Bailey was about to say, "That's not fair," when she noticed Sparrow wheeling toward the Message Stump. She grabbed Goldie's leash and followed.

"Look," said Sparrow, "another message."

Bailey found the Morse code deciphering paper that they left under a rock near the stump.

"What does it say?" asked Sparrow.

Bailey studied the letters. "W-A-T-C-H. It spells 'watch,' " she said.

Before Bailey could translate the remaining words, Goldie put her paws on the stump and knocked away the rest of the sticks and stones.

"Oh, no," said Bailey. "Goldie, why did you do that? Now we don't know what we're supposed to watch for. The twins will be mad."

Goldie whined and licked Bailey's hand. Her ears flicked, and she sniffed the air.

"What is it, girl?" Bailey looked around.

"I don't see anything," said Sparrow, "but something might be watching us. Let's go back."

"Shhh," said Bailey. In the distance she could hear the faint baying of hunting dogs. Goldie strained on her leash.

"Oh, no, you don't," said Bailey, tugging. "You're my dog now."

"Let's go back," urged Sparrow. "I know something's watching us. I'm scared. And it won't fit in my pocket."

"Everything's okay," said Bailey, but she didn't sound convinced.

32

Not Listening

"There was another message on the stump," Sparrow told Fred. He was straightening out a coil of rope on the grass to see how long it was. Noah was examining pulleys, and Duck was measuring pieces of netting that they found in the hayloft of the barn.

"Just enough," said Duck. "Perfect."

"The message spelled 'W-A-T-C-H,' " Sparrow continued.

"Watch what?" said Fred. "Hey, this looks like enough rope. This is going to work."

Sparrow looked at Bailey and shook her head. "I must be invisible," she whispered.

"Me, too," whispered Bailey with a grin.

"If we're invisible, then we can talk, and they won't hear us," said Sparrow.

"Good idea. Let's talk about a music party that Sugar wants to have," said Bailey. "Everyone is supposed to play an instrument."

"One of my foster fathers taught me how to play the comb and tissue paper, but it tickles my lips," said Sparrow.

"Sugar says that you can play one of the jugs in the jug band, or maybe you can make noise with a pan and spoon."

Bailey looked at the boys. Noah and Duck were busy tying the net to the ropes and running the rope through the pulleys. Next to the nets was a large wooden box that Fred was nailing together. The box had a large opening in one side.

"If you put something you trap in there, won't it just get out through the hole?" Bailey asked Fred. Fred pounded harder without answering.

"Jug. I want to play a jug," said Sparrow. "I saw a jug band once. What'll we eat?" She said the word "eat" extra loud to see if she could get the boys' attention.

"Sugar said we can make rollout cookies in the shape of notes and instruments—she has special cookie cutters from Christmas—and maybe lemonade."

"COOKIES!" said Sparrow very loudly. "I love to make COOKIES." That they heard.

"Who's got cookies?" asked Noah. "Hey, Sparrow, could you go to the house and see if

Mom has any? I'm hungry." He went back to tying the rope. "We also need a ball of string. It's on the kitchen counter."

Sparrow looked at Bailey. "I didn't hear anyone talking. Did you?"

"Nope," said Bailey. "They must be invisible. I'll get the string for them and cookies for us."

33

Setting the trap

By the time Bailey came back from the house with the string, the boys had suspended the large net from the branches of four trees near the Message Stump. They stuck leaves in the net to disguise it.

Then, following Duck's directions, Fred stretched a rope across the path at ankle level. He attached another rope to it and tied it to the net. Duck said if something came along the path and tripped on the rope, the net would fall and catch the monster.

At the same time, the monster-detector would be activated when the rope fell. A string connected to it would tug on the alarm in Noah's room. Noah would wake up Fred, and they would run outside to see what was in the trap.

"Perfect," said Duck. "I know it's going to work."

"Cool," said Sparrow, eating her cookie.

Bailey wasn't so sure that it would work. It had never been tested out.

"Here, unwind this and take it back toward the house," said Noah. He tied one end to the detector and handed the string ball to Bailey. She walked slowly toward the house, being careful not to get it tangled in Miss Bekka's raspberry bushes.

She was almost to the house when Clover darted out from under the porch and tripped over the string. Her legs became tangled in it, and before Bailey could catch her, Clover raced across the yard, yanking and pulling at the string. Bailey heard the boys yelling at her, but she couldn't catch the yelping dog. Finally, the string snapped and Clover ran back under the porch.

"That was close," said Fred. "If Noah hadn't grabbed the detector, the string would have pulled it over. Tie a good knot at the break, Bailey."

Noah followed Bailey this time, kicking a little dirt and leaves over the string so it wouldn't be easily seen.

He told Bailey to stand near the bushes under his window on the second floor and went in the house. In a few minutes Noah opened his window, removed the screen, and stepped gingerly out on the porch roof.

"Toss it to me," he said.

Bailey hurled the ball of string. It reached Noah on the first try. Noah carried it into his room.

"Now, we're ready for anything," said Noah when he came back outside.

"All we have to do is wait," said Duck. "I hope we catch it before I have to go back home."

34

Voice in the Woods

Bailey and Goldie wandered slowly back to Sugar's house where dinner was waiting. Duck wanted to stay longer at Keswick Inn to make sure that the alarm in Noah's room would work. That meant that she and Sugar would have to come get him so he wouldn't have to walk home in the dark.

Duck had been annoying during most of his visit, but Bailey had to hand it to him. His inventions seemed to be working.

Goldie stopped and put her nose in the air. Her ears twitched. What did she hear? What did she smell? Bailey tightened her grip on the leash. There was a crackling sound to the right of her, and then another. Goldie whined. Bailey shivered in the warm evening air. More crackling and snapping. Closer. Closer.

"Who's there?" asked Bailey.

Silence. Then, holly branches moved.

"We're leaving," said a small husky voice.

Bailey jumped. "Who are you?" she asked.

"Not a monster, like you think," said the voice.

Bailey grabbed Goldie's collar. The dog sat down at her side. "I don't know who you are."

"I wrote you messages," the voice said. "In code. Then you came down to where we lived in the old car. You seem nice. Now we've got to go because of the boys and the bear."

Bailey was confused. "Why are you leaving? Nobody's bothering you." She peered into the bushes, but she still couldn't see anything.

"The boys are setting traps. I know because I've been watching them. Mom's afraid they'll come back to our camp and cause trouble. We're almost out of food. The bear got some of it, and my sister's sick. I'm scared."

"Come with me," said Bailey. "My grandmother will help. Her name is Sugar."

"Can't," said the boy. "Mom'll be upset. I gotta go. Bye."

Bailey heard steps going farther into the woods. "C'mon, Goldie. We've got to find Sugar," she said. The dog and girl took off at a run toward home.

35

Telling Sugar

Sugar was talking on her cell phone in the kitchen when Bailey pounded up the back steps. She motioned to her grandmother that she needed to talk with her. "It's urgent," Bailey wrote on a piece of paper and held it up. Sugar quickly snapped her phone closed and said, "What's up? You're all out of breath."

Bailey said, "People are living in the woods and they need your help. They're leaving tonight."

"Slow down," said Sugar, "and tell me the whole story from the beginning."

Bailey started with the messages on the hickory stump.

"Interesting," said her grandmother.

Then she told Sugar about the messages, the monster, and going into the woods and discovering the family. She mentioned the maroon sneakers on the clothesline, but decided not to tell Sugar about the boys' trap. All of a sudden it seemed stupid.

"Well," said Sugar. "I'm glad you finally told me about the family, but I wish you had done so sooner so we could have helped them. They may be gone before we get there. It's already twilight."

"The mother said she didn't want help. I asked her," said Bailey.

"That may be true," said Sugar, "but I would like to try. Woman to woman."

Sugar took two brown shopping bags out of the pantry and said, "Let's quickly fill these bags with food a camping family can use, like powdered milk and peanut butter."

When the bags were full, Bailey and Sugar put them in the back of the pickup and drove back toward Keswick Inn. Goldie sat on the floor, but put her front feet in Bailey's lap so she could see out the truck window.

Bailey wondered if she had done the right thing. The twins wouldn't think so. The mother of the family in the woods had told her to leave them alone, but the boy who wrote messages wanted help for his family. That was all that mattered at the moment.

Beyond the Keswicks' driveway was the entrance to the dirt road that went down past the campsite in the woods. Sugar drove there first and turned in. She shut off the truck's engine and waited. Sugar appeared to be watching and listening intently.

"What are you doing?" whispered Bailey.

"My guess is that if they're leaving, they'll come by this way. If we block the road, I'll have a chance to talk for a moment."

They waited only ten minutes when Bailey and Sugar heard the sound of a vehicle coming toward them out of the woods. She recognized the station wagon. "That's them," said Bailey.

Sugar flicked her headlights and got out of the truck when the station wagon stopped a few feet from them. "Stay here," she said to Bailey.

The thin woman opened the driver's door and walked toward Sugar. She scowled fiercely as if that might scare her off. Bailey tried to see the faces of the children, but she couldn't.

Sugar's hands moved a lot when she talked. The woman listened. Soon the scowl softened into sadness. The woman pointed to the station wagon and back at the woods.

Sugar took a paper and pen from her pocket. She wrote something and gave the paper to the woman. The woman nodded and shook Sugar's hand. She followed Sugar to the truck and accepted the bags of groceries.

Without looking at Bailey, the woman walked back to her car.

Sugar returned, backed up the truck and said to Bailey, "Let's go."

36

The Trap Springs

"I can't believe you told Sugar about the people," said Noah. "Now we'll never know what they were up to." He dragged a wicker chair across the porch to where Fred, Bailey, and Duck were sitting.

"Bailey did the right thing," said Fred. "We should've told someone sooner."

Bailey was relieved that someone was sticking up for her.

"Sugar said that she told the mother to go to the Dottie-Anna. They're looking for a new cook, and the mother needs a job," said Bailey. "And Sugar's helping them find a place to stay that isn't in the woods."

Noah was silent. He tapped his fingers.

Suddenly Sparrow opened the door and wheeled out. "Hey, guys, I just heard the monster alarm going off in Noah's room. Didn't you hear it? It was pretty loud," she said.

"Wow! The monster-detector works, Duck," said Noah, slapping the younger boy on the back. "You're a genius. Let's go." Fred grabbed a flashlight, and they raced off through the dark yard, ignoring Sparrow's shout of "Wait for me."

The boys stopped a few yards from the Message Stump. The beam from Fred's light searched the trees and then the ground. The net had indeed fallen, and something was growling, squealing, and thrashing inside.

"The monster," whispered Duck dramatically. "Approach with care."

"You know," said Noah. "We never came up with a plan for what to do when we caught something in the trap. What now, dudes?"

Bailey said, "Let's see what it is, and then we can figure things out." With all the commotion in the trap, she wasn't sure how close she wanted to get.

To her surprise, the normally cautious Duck took the lead. They walked quietly behind him, curious about what was caught in the webbing. The net stopped rustling. The creature was waiting for them.

Duck inched closer. "Hey, guys, shine your light in the middle of the net," he whispered.

Fred leaned over Duck's shoulders and aimed the beam.

"Oh, no!" Fred yelled, but it was too late.

"Yikes! Help! Help!" screamed Duck. "It got me. Help!"

"Got me, too," yelled Fred. "I can't see. Outta here."

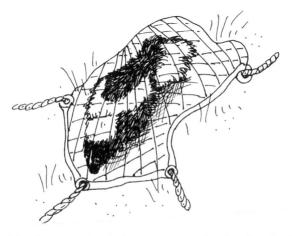

Noah vanished the moment he had inhaled a whiff. Bailey knew she didn't want to hang around another minute, either. She saw Sparrow coming down the path.

"What's going on? Where's everybody going?" shouted Sparrow. Bailey grabbed her wheelchair and turned it around. She pushed her quickly away from the trap.

"What's that awful smell? What happened to Duck and Fred?" asked Sparrow.

"Skunk," said Bailey, laughing. "They caught a skunk. Or rather, a skunk caught them."

She knew it wasn't nice to laugh, but she couldn't help herself.

37

Tomato Juice

Fred and Duck were not allowed in the house until they scrubbed outside with soap mixed with baking soda and then rinsed with the garden hose. Miss Bekka poured thick red tomato juice on their hair to help get rid of the odor. "Pineapple juice works better, but sometimes tomato juice helps," she said.

After a brief discussion, Miss Bekka and Sugar decided to throw away the skunky clothes rather than try to wash out the smell. They quickly bagged the boys' outfits and put them in the back of Sugar's pickup so she could take them to the landfill the next day.

"What'll I wear?" cried Duck. "I can't go around in a towel." Tomato juice trickled down his face.

"We'll loan you clothes, little dude," said Noah. He grinned. "Hey, Mom. We need a picture of Duck and Fred."

"No teasing, Noah," said Miss Bekka. Duck looked relieved.

"Here comes Will with a report on your skunk," Sugar said.

Mr. Will said he'd carefully checked out the trap area. He'd determined that the skunk had managed to crawl out from under the net and had returned to the woods.

"I suppose you 'redheads' have learned a lesson about polecats," Mr. Will said to Duck and Fred. "Suppose so," said Fred. He sounded miserable.

When Duck looked puzzled, Mr. Will said, "Polecat is another name for skunk."

"Skunks are even worse than bugs. My next invention will be a skunk-detector," said Duck. "I hope this smell goes away before my grandfather comes back."

"Pee-you. I'm just glad the skunk didn't get me," said Sparrow, holding her nose.

"Let me tell you something about skunks," said Sugar. "They're really very beneficial animals and they are a great help to gardeners. Skunks eat beetles, slugs, baby rats, mice, and other things that can wreck a garden.

"In fact, when I was at camp as a child, our leader captured one and tamed it. It was very gentle," Sugar added.

"Really?" asked Sparrow.

Duck didn't look convinced.

Mr. Will said, "Skunks are nocturnal and will defend themselves with spray if they think they're being attacked . . . or trapped. They often give a warning before they spray."

Usually the kids would be interested in what Sugar or Mr. Will said about nature. Right now, Fred and Duck, dripping with tomato juice, didn't look like they cared.

Mr. Will sat on the porch steps near the boys. "Now I'd like to hear about this trap and what you'd expected to catch."

38

Upsetting E-mail

Duck muttered about the skunk during the drive home and went up to bed without asking to use the computer. Bailey decided to check her e-mail before turning in for the night. There was one from Norma Jean, and one from her mother.

As always, Norma Jean had questions about Justin. She was one of the few people Bailey knew who really liked him and saw the good in him.

From: pjfish2005@yermail.net>
To: "Bailey"<baileyfish@gmail.com>
Sent: 4:45 p.m.
Subject: What's up

Bailey, I don't like it when you don't write me. What's going on? Did Noah and Justin make up? Did you catch a monster yet? Mom and I went shopping yesterday for school clothes. I can't believe summer is almost over. Did you go shopping yet? Write me. NJ

Bailey replied:

From: "Bailey"<baileyfish@gmail.com>
To: <pjfish2005@yermail.net>
Sent: 9:05 p.m.
Subject: skunk

Guess what? A skunk was in the trap and Fred and Duck got sprayed. They stink. It was very funny. I haven't seen Justin in a few days. I heard his mom went back to work. Sugar and I are going to the Dottie-Anna tomorrow. Duck leaves in a few days. Sugar hasn't said anything about shopping. Bailey

She sent the message, then opened the one from her mother.

From: Mollyf2@travl.net
To: "Bailey"<baileyfish@gmail.com>
Sent: 6 a.m.
Subject: dog

Bailey dearest, I've put some pieces of lava in the mail to you, and a shark's tooth necklace. I think you and your friends will find them interesting. By the way, I didn't mean to upset you about the dog. What I meant was, because you are just living with Sugar for a while, I worry that you are getting too attached to her pets in Virginia. Who knows where we will all be in the next year or so. XXXOOO Mom

Bailey felt as if an earthquake had crumbled the world. What was the matter with her mom? What was she talking about? Sallie, Shadow, and Goldie weren't Sugar's pets—they were

141

hers! Bailey thought for a moment, then wrote:

From: "Bailey"<baileyfish@gmail.com>
To: <Mollyf2@travl.net>
Sent: 9:05 p.m.
Subject: mine

Mom, I told you before that the cats and Goldie are MINE, not Sugar's. I love them and they love me. I won't leave them. Ever.

Bailey wanted to say, "Why do you even care? I think you like Bug Man more than me." What really worried her was that her mother might want to marry Bug Man, and then what would happen? Would her mom make her give up her pets and go to live with Mr. and Mrs. Bug Man in Costa Rica where she didn't even know anyone? A lump closed her throat.

Her worries kept her from hearing Sugar coming into the office.

"Want to sit on the porch for a while?" asked her grandmother.

Bailey gulped back tears, logged off without sending the reply to her mother, and nodded yes.

"I'll fix lemonade," said Sugar.

39

Mahalo

Bailey didn't sleep well. She woke up every few hours and reached out to pet Shadow, Sallie, and Goldie. "I love you," she told the sleeping animals. "I promise that I won't go anywhere without you."

When Bailey looked at the clock, she was surprised that it was already 7:30. She quickly dressed and brushed her hair.

Duck was already downstairs eating cereal. He had a tinge of red around his scalp where the tomato juice hadn't washed out completely.

"We're going to the Dottie-Anna for muffins this morning," said Sugar.

"Please drop me at Keswicks'," said Duck. "We have to clean up the trap and put everything back in the barn."

"Probably have to throw the net away," said Bailey. She poured milk on her cereal. "I bet it still stinks."

"It worked, though," he said. "It really worked."

"That it did," said Sugar with a chuckle.

"Okay, we'll be back in about an hour," said Sugar when they left Duck at Keswick Inn. He ran toward the chicken coop where Sparrow and the boys were waiting for him.

"Duck doesn't seem to be worrying about bugs anymore," said Bailey. "He used to walk slowly to watch out for them."

"I think country life has been good for him," said Sugar.

Within a few minutes they were at the Dottie-Anna. Bailey noticed that Nora Rudd's car was in the side lot where employees parked. Next to it was the beat-up station wagon.

"Looks like Lilo Ashby took my suggestion about looking for a job here," said Sugar. "Let's go see."

"Lilly?" said Bailey.

"No, Lilo—the name of the woman you found in the woods," said Sugar. She opened the door to the Dottie-Anna.

Mrs. Rudd was bustling about the restaurant, pouring coffee and taking orders. She smiled when she saw Bailey and Sugar.

From their usual seats at the counter, Bailey could see through an opening into the kitchen. She saw Lilo Ashby talking to the owners. Mrs. Kamaka handed her an apron and pointed to the stove.

"Ah, Lilo's going to get a chance to be the new cook," said Sugar. "She told me she had restaurant experience when she lived in Honolulu."

"She's from Hawaii?" asked Bailey.

"A long time ago," said Sugar. "So are the Kamakas."

"What? They're not foreigners from another country?" Bailey said with surprise.

Sugar looked at her with a puzzled expression.

"Justin heard . . . oh, never mind," said Bailey when Mrs. Kamaka came to the counter. She was beaming.

"Mahalo—thank you—for finding us a cook and one from our own state!" she said. "And when Nora Rudd's boy is a little older, we may be able to put him to work here, too. Nora says he's a hard worker. Mahalo."

Bailey was astonished.

Mrs. Kamaka said in her lilting voice with the slight accent, "Now what would you like today?"

"Let's split an order of your french toast," said Sugar. "With extra strawberries, please."

"Mahalo," said Bailey when Mrs. Kamaka brought breakfast to the table. "Did I pronounce that right?"

Mrs. Kamaka nodded. "Yes, and I'll be glad to teach you more words from our native Hawaiian language sometime. For example, my first name, Mele, means 'song.' "

"Mele is a beautiful name," said Bailey.

40

Mr. Jefferson's Ice Cream

"How many people are coming to our Thomas Jefferson party?" Bailey asked. She helped Sugar unpack twenty glasses she'd bought at a yard sale to use for the musical glasses. They had already set up the jugs on a table on the back porch and filled them with different amounts of water.

"If everyone shows up—I think, about thirty. Maybe forty," said Sugar. "We'll have plenty of food and more than enough musical instruments." She motioned to the jugs and glasses.

Sugar and Bailey had gotten up very early, when the first streamers of pink and purple light filled the eastern sky.

"Next, we'll work on the Presidential Ice Cream," said Sugar. "It'll need time to freeze."

"I made up a Lewis and Clark treasure hunt game," said Bailey. "It involves exploration. I don't know if the bigger kids will play games, though."

"You never know," said Sugar, "especially if we offer prizes. I have a box of odds and ends that might work for giveaways."

Sugar tied an apron over her jeans and flattened Thomas Jefferson's recipe for vanilla ice cream on the kitchen counter. The recipe had been rewritten from his original so that it was easier to understand. It had only four ingredients: cream, egg yolks, sugar, and a vanilla bean.

Bailey measured the sugar and combined it with the egg yolks. Sugar showed her how to set up the double boiler, with the lower pan for boiling water and the upper one for cooking the ingredients.

Just then, Duck padded into the room carrying Shadow. "You guys are up early," he said. "I want to help."

Shadow jumped to the floor, ran to the refrigerator, and meowed. Duck opened the door and poured milk for the cat. He then climbed on a stool so he could reach the cereal and fixed his breakfast.

"How about decorating the musical cookies?" asked Sugar. "I baked them in the shapes of a note, drum, guitar, saxophone, and piano."

"Sure," said Duck. "I've never done that before. Grandmother and her helper always decorated the cookies because Grandmother said I might make a mess."

"I know you'll do a great job," said Sugar. She moved the stool next to the counter so Duck could easily reach the cream cheese frosting and colored sugar crystals.

"Wash your hands first," said Sugar. "And when you're done, you can lick the bowl."

Duck's eyes were bright with excitement. He quickly finished his breakfast, and scrubbed his hands. "I'm ready."

Bailey poured the cream and added vanilla. She watched Duck carefully smooth the frosting, then sprinkle the colors, raisins, or cinnamon drops. She smiled when she saw him pop a piece of broken cookie in his mouth.

When the ice cream ingredients were heated, Sugar helped Bailey pour the mixture through a cheese cloth to strain out the lumps. After it had cooled, they poured it into an ice cream maker that Sugar had bought at a yard sale, and let it churn. The mixture would then go into the freezer until the party.

"You've never decorated cookies before, and I've never made ice cream," said Bailey.

"My cookies are the best," said Duck.

41

Singing Glasses

The Keswicks were the first to arrive. Miss Bekka brought a bucket of sunflowers and zinnias and two raspberry pies. The boys carried their bongo drum and guitar. Sparrow held a tambourine that Miss Bekka helped her make out of a tin can lid and bells.

Mr. Will and the boys lifted a large box covered with a quilt out of the van's trunk, and set it in the side yard.

"What's that?" asked Bailey.

"Something to sit on. A box seat, get it?" said Fred. "We thought you might need extra seats for the party."

Mr. Will set the wheelchair on the porch. "What are those glasses for?" Sparrow asked.

"For music," said Bailey. "I'll show you." She moistened her finger and rubbed it around the rim of one glass, and then another. Each made a different ringing note.

"I want to do it," said Sparrow. "That's music like angels would make."

Mr. Will placed a large pillow in her chair so she could reach the glasses. Sparrow watched Bailey make the music again, and then tried it herself. "Did you hear me? I did it!"

Sparrow tried every glass she could reach.

"I heard that President Thomas Jefferson was very interested in the musical sounds made by rubbing the glasses. So we're going to try them today, and we're also going to play jugs," said Bailey.

Fred and Noah spotted the jugs and blew across the top openings.

"Neat," said Sparrow. "I want to try a jug."

Bailey handed her one. "We might be able to figure out a simple song—and play it one note at a time."

"If you don't laugh while you're doing it," said Mr. Will. He blew across the largest of the jugs, and it made a deep sound, like the note was coming from inside a giant hole.

The house and yard filled with friends and neighbors. Mrs. Rudd had to work late, so Justin brought his little sisters. At first he refused to come in the house, but then Mr. Will and Noah went over to where he was standing under the apple tree. Bailey watched Noah say something and put out his hand.

After a moment, Justin nodded and shook Noah's hand. He took his sisters' hands followed Noah to the house.

"Is Mrs. Ashby coming with her kids?" asked Bailey.

"I invited her, and the Kamakas, but they may all be working. It's pizza night at the Dottie-Anna," said Sugar.

"What's going to happen to the Ashbys?" asked Bailey. "The kids, I mean."

"The family's problems won't be solved quickly, but Mrs. Ashby has a job, and people from the county are helping them now," said Sugar. "They're safe, sleeping indoors, and have plenty to eat. Now, speaking of food, let's have a Monticello feast."

"Thomas Jefferson really liked vegetables," said Bailey.

Duck made a face.

"He experimented with different kinds of vegetables such as squash from Italy and beans collected by Lewis and Clark on their expedition," she added. "And he really liked salads."

"So our party menu today comes from Monticello," said Sugar.

Sugar and Bailey served macaroni and cheese, chicken pudding, beef stew, a big green salad, peas, something called "good pudding" made from bread, milk, apples, sugar and spices, plus macaroni pudding, and finally vanilla ice cream.

Duck proudly presented his trays of beautifully decorated musical-shaped lemon cookies, and Bailey scooped the somewhat mushy, but delicious, ice cream into paper bowls. Everyone agreed that the best part was the desserts.

"I may have to use some of these recipes at Keswick Inn," said Miss Bekka. "This food is yummy."

42

Goldie's House

"That sure was fun," said Bailey. She poured water out of the glasses, dried them off, and carefully put them back in the cardboard box on the back steps. She still couldn't figure out why the boys were acting so strangely.

"We have one more surprise for you," announced Noah. "My dear brother Fred and dear Cousin Duck and I have been working on something special. Stay in your seats, please."

Bailey sat back down on the large quilt-covered box near Fern and Sparrow.

"Stand up, Bailey, and remove the cloth from your box seat, please," said Noah. Duck did a drum roll with wooden spoons on an upside-down bucket.

Bailey yanked the cloth. Under it was just the box with the hole that Fred had been making in the barn. So what was the big deal? Bailey tried not to seem too disappointed.

Mr. Will said, "Let's have a closer look." He tipped the box so that it stood up properly, and turned it around. The box had a pointed roof. Above the hole was a bright yellow sign that read: GOLDIE.

The boys had made a doghouse for Goldie.

"Don't you like it?" asked Duck. "I designed it."

"It was my idea," said Noah.

"And I built most of it," said Fred.

"You knew her name all along?" asked Bailey, remembering the times they called her dog anything but her real name.

"Just goofing on you," said Noah. "You're much too easy to tease. Do you like it?"

"It's wonderful," said Bailey. "Goldie sleeps in the house with me, though."

Duck said, "We know, but if she's outside and wants to take a nap while you're reading, now she'll have a nice house. You can put straw inside for a bed."

Bailey showed Goldie the entrance, and the dog went in as if she knew the house was hers.

"Thanks," Bailey said. How could she have thought her friends didn't care about her and her dog?

43

Following the Hounds

Bailey's room hadn't cooled down much during the night. Her pillow was damp with sweat. She dreamed that she heard a pack of dogs calling Goldie's name and that she and Goldie chased after them in the moonlight.

When she and Goldie caught up to the dog pack in a silvery clearing, Bailey saw that the hounds had treed a fox the color of tomato juice.

The hounds weren't interested in hurting the fox—it was just a game of tag.

Soon the fox was chasing all of them, and the game quickly turned into hide-and-seek. When it was Goldie's turn to hide, the moon slipped into the horizon and parts of the Milky Way crumbled after it. Bailey's dream was so vivid that it seemed real when she awoke.

Without opening her eyes, Bailey kicked off the sheet and reached over the side of the bed, like she always did, to pet Goldie. No dog. She rolled over and looked down. Goldie wasn't on her dog bed. She sat up quickly and looked around. Goldie wasn't in the room. Bailey changed into her shorts and blue T-shirt, ran her fingers through her hair, and rushed down the stairs. Sugar was sipping coffee while she waited for the toast to pop up.

"Where's Goldie?" asked Bailey.

"I thought you went outside with her for an early walk," said Sugar. "The screen door was partly open when I came out of my office for more coffee."

"Oh, no!" said Bailey. She looked around for her sneakers. "Maybe I wasn't dreaming about dogs running in the woods. They must have been real ones. We need to find her."

"Uh-oh. I heard the hounds while I was at my computer," said Sugar. "They were close and seemed to be heading west. I hope Goldie isn't trying to join them."

Bailey tied her sneakers and grabbed Goldie's leash.

"I'll leave a note for Duck, then I'll follow you," called Sugar. "I'll hurry."

Bailey burst out the door.

44

Brave Rescue

Bailey dashed across the backyard to the path through the woods that went to the west—land where pine trees were grown for the timber harvest. Hunters had permission to use the land during different seasons. Sugar had told her that hunting was necessary to thin the deer population.

Bailey wasn't familiar with this path. She stopped for a moment to listen. At first all she heard in the humid morning air was the raucous sound of crows. Then, far in the distance, were barking hounds. Bailey ran harder, her heart pounding. She stopped to catch her breath. The pack seemed to be doubling back her way. She ran again, not caring if branches snapped across her arms leaving little bloody scratches. *Goldie, I'm coming.*

The path came to a clearing and a dirt road with deep tire ruts from logging trucks. When

Bailey stopped for breath again she saw a blue-green pickup parked on the edge of the road and a large man leaning against it. The bed of the pickup contained cages for transporting hunting dogs.

Bailey thought, *Maybe he's seen Goldie.* She was about to ask when the barking became louder and the pack came into view. *Oh no! Goldie's with them.*

The man whistled for his dogs and all but one jumped into the truck. He turned and saw Goldie.

"What the—?" the man said angrily. "I thoughts you's dead by now, ya no good dumb thang. Ruinin' my pack again. I'll teach ya."

When Goldie heard his voice, she whimpered and lay down, creeping toward him on her belly.

The man reached for a heavy stick. "I cut you loose, stupid. Couldn't hunt. Couldn't do nuttin' right." He raised the club above the dog's head.

"No," screamed Bailey. "Don't hurt my dog! Goldie, come here!"

"What the—?" the man yelled. He brandished the stick at the quivering dog. Hearing Bailey's voice, Goldie thumped her tail. Bailey rushed over and wrapped her arms around her dog's neck. She snapped the leash on Goldie's collar and hunched over her.

"Please don't hurt her. She's my dog now." Bailey couldn't believe that her voice had any braveness left in it. She was shaking inside.

The man took a step toward them. He hadn't dropped the stick. His face was filled with surprise and annoyance.

"Outta the way, missy," he said. Bailey didn't budge. The man stepped closer. Bailey clung to Goldie's neck. Their hearts pounded as one.

"Put the stick down, Emule Hathaway," said a familiar voice. "We need to have a talk." It was Sugar.

The man dropped the stick and wiped sweat off his forehead. His feet did not move.

"Miss Sugar, this is not what it seems," he said. "I meant no harm to the dog."

"Is she one of yours?" asked Sugar.

"Was," said the man. "Dumb thang ran off during hunting season last December."

"Oh? Without a collar?" asked Sugar. "The hunting dog just unbuckled her collar, dropped it on the ground, and ran away into the woods? I doubt that very much."

Emule Hathaway looked at his heavy, unlaced boots.

Sugar continued. "The dog was hurt and near starvation when Mrs. Chaffee took her in. Mrs. Chaffee posted notices and tried to have someone claim her. Put up signs everywhere. Did you see the posters with the dog's picture at the post office, Emule? Did you?" Sugar stepped between the man, the still-crouching Bailey, and the cowering dog.

The man didn't answer. Finally, he said, "She's a no-good hunting dog, and she mixed up my other dogs. A hound's got to hunt to earn her keep."

Sugar cleared her throat.

"Maybe I could make an exception," he said. He took a step toward them.

Bailey was suddenly afraid that the man would be shamed into taking Goldie back. She looked up at her grandmother's face with alarm. Sugar stared thoughtfully at Emule Hathaway.

"Tell you what," Sugar said. "I don't think you want me to report you for abandoning this 'no-good hunting dog,' as you call her. She's lived with us for several weeks and makes a fine pet for my granddaughter. We want to keep her."

"I 'spose," grumbled the man.

"And the second thing is, I want you to hunt where our dog can't hear your pack of hounds. There're lots of woods in the county. Run your dogs somewhere far from here. Thirdly, don't abandon any other dogs. Take care of them and find them homes if you don't want them."

"Miss Sugar, that's asking a lot," said Emule Hathaway. His eyes narrowed. He turned his head to the left and spit.

Sugar took her cell phone out of her pocket and punched in three numbers.

"Wait," he said. "Like ya said. There's lots of woods in the county. Lots of places to run my hounds and hunt. Don't need to hunt here."

He looked at Bailey and said, "The no-good thang is yours, missy." He kicked the big stick out of his way and returned to his pickup, locked the dog cages, and squealed his tires as he drove off.

Bailey stood up and hugged Sugar until Goldie squeezed between them.

"Now you're my forever dog," Bailey said.

Goldie licked her fingers and rolled on her back for a belly rub.

"C'mon, girls," said Sugar. "That's enough of an adventure before breakfast. I think the toast is cold, and we need to get home to help Duck pack."

45

Country Clothes

"I won't be needing these anymore," said Duck. He placed his country clothes in a brown sack on the kitchen table. He looked starchy and stiff in the outfit he wore when he had arrived at Sugar's house just three weeks earlier. His hair was slicked down with water, but he was no longer pale. His arms, legs and face were tanned from being outside.

"I suppose they'll be too small for you by the time you come back for another visit," said Sugar.

"If my grandmother lets me come back. She's so strict. Don't tell her about the skunk." Duck was silent for a moment, then said, "I really wish you were my . . ." He stopped talking and turned away.

"I'm an honorary grandmother for several people," said Sugar. "That means I'll always love you even if I'm not your official grandmother."

Duck turned and threw his arms around Sugar. Finally, he said, "The clothes were really good. Thanks."

"I'm proud of you, Duck. You tried new things and learned to not be so afraid of the outdoors," said Sugar. "I know we'll see you again."

"And you're a good inventor," said Bailey. "You have really good ideas."

Duck nodded. "Noah called me 'little dude.' I didn't know he really liked me."

"Everybody likes you," said Bailey.

"Hey, e-mail me if the bear comes back," Duck added.

"Sure," Bailey said. She was surprised that Duck felt so bad about leaving, especially when he hadn't wanted to stay in the first place. She was even more surprised that she was sorry to see him go home.

Goldie followed Duck upstairs when he went to get his suitcase. When he returned, Duck asked Sugar if he could borrow some of the books that she bought at the yard sale.

"Of course," she said. "That would make me very happy."

Duck selected four books and tucked them in the outside pocket of his suitcase. Just then the doorbell rang.

"It's your grandfather," said Bailey.

Cousin Max chuckled when he saw Duck. "Well, look at you. I think you're taller and it would appear that the country has agreed with you."

Duck smiled. "It was fun. Do you want to see sketches of my inventions? Sugar let me tape them on a door in my room."

"No time, buddy," said Max. "Your grandmother can't be home alone very long until she is stronger. We need to get going right away."

Duck's smile vanished.

"Max, I'd like to visit with you for a moment. Come into my office," said Sugar.

"Okay," said Max. He followed her and closed the door behind him.

"I wonder what that's about," said Duck. He sounded worried.

Bailey wasn't sure, but she guessed that Sugar would be trying to help Duck somehow. Bailey opened the cookie jar and held it out to her cousin. He took two peanut butter cookies. Bailey put the jar back on the counter and handed Duck a stick and a stone.

"What're these?" Duck asked.

"They're from the Message Stump. Part of the Morse code. They'll help you remember our adventures."

Duck smiled and tucked them in his pocket. "Thanks. I'll put them in my treasure box."

The talking stopped in the other room and Max and Sugar returned to the kitchen. Max said, "Well, Duck, before we head back to the city, I think you need to change into your country clothes. They're much more comfortable in the summer, and we'll go to the park after we check on your grandmother." He ran his hand through Duck's wavy hair. "We'll save the other clothes for school and eating out."

"Really?" Duck looked up at his grandfather in astonishment. He hesitated only for a moment, then grabbed the brown sack and ran back upstairs.

When he came back down, Duck was dressed in his cutoff shorts, a yellow T-shirt that used to belong to Fred, and tan sneakers with holes in the toes. "Are you sure it's okay?"

Max beamed. "Yes, buddy. Now we've got to go. But first, show me the bear's paw prints. I hear you've had a big furry visitor this summer." Duck actually grinned.

Duck hugged Sugar again, and waved good-bye twice to Bailey—once in the kitchen, and once from the car.

"What were you talking about with his grandfather?" asked Bailey when their car was out of sight.

"As honorary grandmother, I felt obliged to make a few suggestions to Max. I urged him to let Duck invent, create and get dirty sometimes outdoors," said Sugar. "Max agreed. He said he'll work on it with Duck's grandmother, now that she's going to feel better. That's a start."

"I'm so glad you're *my* grandmother," said Bailey.

Sugar gave her one of her famous bear hugs. "Now, what shall we do today?"

"Let's have an adventure," said Bailey. "With Goldie."

"Now that Emule and his hounds are gone, I think it's safe to take her for a run in Contrary Woods," said Sugar.

Hearing her name, Goldie grabbed her leash and pranced to the door.

"You're the best dog ever," said Bailey. She turned and gave her grandmother another hug.

"Mahalo, Sugar. Thanks for letting me have Goldie," Bailey said.

Discussion Questions

1. Sparrow and Bailey are both afraid of a bear in the woods. What does Sugar tell Bailey to do if she is afraid of something? How does this help Sparrow? Has anyone ever given you advice about how to face your fear of something? What did they tell you?

2. Why is Duck at first unhappy at Sugar's house? What does he want to do that he cannot do there? By the end of the book, how has he changed? Do you think he will change back to his old self when he returns to the city? Why or why not?

3. Bailey gets e-mails from both of her parents. What do her parents say? What do they *not* say? Why do you think the e-mails make her angry? Why doesn't she want to answer them?

4. Noah, Fred, Sparrow, Bailey, and Duck think of many possibilities for names for Dog.

Why does Bailey finally name her Goldie? Did you ever name a pet? How did you decide what to call it? How did you get your own name? How do you feel about your name? Would you want to be called Duck?

5. Bailey knows she worries about many things, but she says Duck is "the king of worriers." Do you agree? Can you list three things that worry Bailey? Can you name three things that worry Duck? Write about one thing that worries you.

6. At first, Noah and Fred make fun of Duck's invention ideas. Bailey doesn't like their tone. By the time Duck is ready to go home, he tells Bailey, "Noah called me 'little dude.' I didn't know he really liked me." At what point in the story do Noah and Fred change their opinion about Duck? Why do you think they all become friends?

7. Why is Nora Rudd afraid she will lose her job? Justin seems worried, too. Why do we know he is worried?

8. Why do Bailey and Sparrow feel invisible around the boys? Why do the boys keep getting Dog's new name wrong? Why do the boys not include the girls in their plan to catch the monster? How do they apologize?

9. What if the homeless children who live in the car had spent a day, a week, or a month with Sugar. How would Sugar help them? What adventures would she take them on?

10. Write the conversation Sugar has with Lilo Ashby in the woods.

11. Why would Goldie return to the pack of hunting dogs when her owner, Emule Hathaway, treated her so badly? Do dogs remember things? How do you know Goldie remembers Emule was mean to her?

12. What did you think the boys were going to catch in the trap? What if they had caught the bear?

13. Did you ever think of, or make, an invention? Tell about an invention you would like to make.

14. The story does not tell us how Sugar knows Emule Hathaway. What if they went to junior high school together? Make up a story about Sugar and Emule when they were kids. What kind of little boy do you think Emule was?

15. Do you have any honorary grandmas, aunts, or uncles? Tell the story of how you came to adopt them. Describe a grandfather you would want to adopt as your "honorary" one.

Web Sites

Thomas Jefferson

http://classroom.monticello.org

http://www.foodsiteoftheday.com/thomas_jefferson.htm

http://www.americaslibrary.gov/cgi-bin/page.cgi/aa/presidents/jefferson/home_1

http://cti.itc.virginia.edu/~meg3c/classes/tcc313/200Rprojs/jefferson_invent/invent.html

http://wiki.monticello.org/mediawiki/index.php/Musical_Glasses

Lewis and Clark

http://classroom.monticello.org/kids/resources/home/4/

Morse code

http://www.onlineconversion.com/morse_code.htm

http://freenet.msp.mn.us/people/calguire/morse.html

From Sugar's Bookshelf

All about Famous Inventors and Their Inventions, by Fletcher Pratt

Boxcar Children, The, by Gertrude Chandler Warner

Cooking in the Young Republic, 1780–1850, by Patricia B. Mitchell

Dangerous Book for Boys, The, by Gonn and Hal Iggulden

Jerry Todd and the Purring Egg, by Leo Edwards

Monticello: A Guidebook, by the Thomas Jefferson Foundation

Lewis and Clark, by George Sullivan

Mr. Popper's Penguins, by Richard and Florence Atwater

Rootabaga Stories, by Carl Sandburg

Sideways Stories from Wayside School, by Louis Sachar

Thomas Jefferson's Cook Book, edited by Marie Kimball

Glossary

black bear: The most common bear in North America. They eat berries, nuts, seeds, leaves and also rodents, fish, and meat. The smallest adults can weigh 300 pounds.

dumbwaiter: A small elevator that takes food from one floor to another. At Monticello, it carried only wine bottles. Food was carried up the stairs by servants and put on the revolving serving door or on a serving cart (also called a dumbwaiter), and wheeled next to the guests. "Dumb" means silent.

expedition: A journey made for specific reasons.

explorers: People who travel to learn more about a region, its geography, wildlife, and people.

extruder: A machine that squeezes a thick liquid or paste, like pasta dough, out of a small opening.

foreigner: A person from another country.

Monticello: Italian for "Little Mountain." Monticello was the home and plantation of Thomas Jefferson.

moldboard plow: Thomas Jefferson invented the moldboard of least resistance plow. The plow's curved front (moldboard) was very light and easy to pull. Jefferson was awarded a gold medal by France's Society of Agriculture for the design.

Morse code: Invented by Samuel F. B. Morse (1791–1872) in 1832 for use by the first telegraph in 1836. He sent a message from Washington, D.C., to Baltimore. The code is used by ships and can be sent by sound or light. Besides being an inventor, Morse was a painter.

polygraph: An early letter-copying device with two pens.

pudding: A soft dessert that is creamy or cake-like.

spherical sundial: Another of Thomas Jefferson's inventions, this sundial, instead of being flat, was shaped like a globe.

wheel cipher: Jefferson invented the wheel cipher with twenty-six wooden disks, one for each letter of the alphabet. The letters spun on a metal pin, and words could be scrambled or unscrambled to create or decode messages.

President Thomas Jefferson

Thomas Jefferson, the third president of the United States, was born in 1743 in Shadwell, Virginia, near present-day Charlottesville. Jefferson served as president for two terms, from 1801 to 1809, and was also Virginia's governor from 1779 to 1781. His public service also included representation in the Continental Congress and the House of Delegates.

James L. Dick's portrait of Thomas Jefferson, courtesy of the Thomas Jefferson Foundation /Monticello.

A brilliant man, Jefferson wrote (drafted) the Declaration of Independence that was

Thomas Jefferson designed his home at Monticello, near Charlottesville, Virginia, on 5,000 acres he inherited from his father. The house is surrounded by vegetable and flower gardens. Jefferson was curious about various species and experimented with new

farming techniques. Above, tourists enter the front door of Monticello for a tour of the house. At the left is Jefferson's grave, located in a family cemetery on the property. The grave is seen through a black-and-gold wrought-iron gate. The words he chose for his grave read: "Author of the Declaration of Independence, of the Statute of Virginia for Religious Freedom, and Father of the University of Virginia."

adopted on July 4, 1776. This document proclaimed that "all men are created equal" and have the right to "life, liberty and the pursuit of happiness." He died fifty years to the day of its adoption, on July 4, 1826.

Besides being one of America's Founding Fathers, Thomas Jefferson was a diplomat to France, was elected to Congress and served as secretary of state, and vice president. He sent the Lewis and Clark expedition to explore the west, and designed and planned the University of Virginia in Charlottesville.

His home, Monticello, is near the original family homestead in Shadwell.

While in Europe, Jefferson learned about new foods, such as pasta, and brought recipes and a chef back to Monticello. His inventive mind made him look at ways to adapt inventions and to come up with three of his own.

Lewis and Clark

President Jefferson wanted to learn more about the large territory west of the Mississippi that the government purchased for $15 million. He sent Meriwether Lewis and William Clark to explore the area and report back.

Like Jefferson, Lewis was born in Abemarle County, Virginia, and they were good friends. Clark was a friend of Lewis's.

Jefferson proposed the expedition to learn about the Native-American peoples, animals and routes to the Pacific. The expedition discovered about 100 animals that had not been known before to settlers on the East Coast.

The expedition left from St. Louis, Missouri, on May 14, 1804. The explorers kept journals, so that details of the exciting trip are available today. They carried large peace medals as a gift from Jefferson to the Native-Americans, and to let them know that the territory in which they lived had changed hands from France to the United States.

Lewis and Clark traveled more than 8,000 miles during their two-year journey. Along the way, soldiers and rivermen returned to Washington with nine boxes for the president. The boxes contained antlers, skins, and horns, and even a live prairie dog. Many items from the exploration are on display at Monticello.

The explorers were helped in their journey by a Shoshone woman named Sacagawea ("Bird Woman"). She traveled with the expedition and translated for Lewis and Clark.

After the explorers returned in 1806, Meriwether Lewis became the governor of the Louisiana Territory, and William Clark became the territory's brigadier general. In 1813 Clark was named governor of the Missouri Territory and superintendent of Indian Affairs.

Jefferson's Inventions

Thomas Jefferson's curious mind led him to create three inventions of his own and to make improvements or experiment with inventions and gadgets made by other people.

Below is a picture of a replica of a moldboard plow. The moldboard is the part attached to the handles. This plow cuts into the dirt more easily than others did at the time. Plows were pulled by horses, oxen, or mules and were steered by people. This invention making the job easier would be welcome.

Used by permission of the Thomas Jefferson Foundation / Monticello.

Another invention is the wheel cipher. Notice the alphabet letters on each wooden wheel that can be rotated to create codes. The first picture shows the wheel cipher when it is put together. The second picture shows four disks removed so that you can see how it is constructed. The twenty-six numbered wheels rotate on an iron rod.

Used by permission of the Thomas Jefferson Foundation / Monticello.

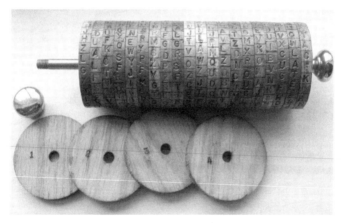

How do you think Thomas Jefferson deciphered codes or wrote in code using this invention?

Thomas Jefferson's third invention was a spherical sundial in the shape of the Earth. The one pictured on page 182 is a replica displayed at Monticello. Jefferson marked the North and South poles and the equator and

This picture of the replica of the spherical sundial is used by permission of the Thomas Jefferson Foundation / Monticello.

meridian (a circle of the Earth going through the poles). The meridian's shadow told the time. The sundial was made from the top part of a column.

Jefferson and Food

Thomas Jefferson liked to eat and try lots of different kinds of foods. He brought recipes back to Monticello from his travels in France. Many kinds of vegetables were grown at Monticello, and Jefferson often preferred vegetables to meat. When he lived in France, he became interested in how to make macaroni and drew a picture of a machine. Macaroni recipes were also prepared at Monticello.

There is no proof, however, that Jefferson came up with the original recipe for macaroni and cheese, even though it is included in a Monticello cookbook of the time. The recipe for macaroni and cheese is much like today's: Break two cups of macaroni into small pieces, cook until tender. Add about one-quarter pound of cheese and butter and bake in a medium oven until the cheese is melted.

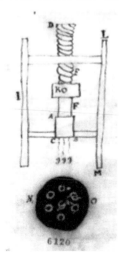

Credit: Thomas Jefferson's drawing of a macaroni machine and instructions for making pasta, ca. 1787 (Thomas Jefferson Papers. 1787. Words and Deeds in American History: Selected Documents Celebrating the Manuscript Division's First 100 Years, Library of Congress.)
The circle with holes at the bottom shows how pasta dough would be squeezed into noodles.

Another recipe is for macaroni pudding. It involves cooking one-eighth cup of macaroni in a pint of milk until tender. Add five eggs, three-fourths cup of sugar, and a teaspoon of lemon juice or vanilla. Bake one hour at 350°.

Jefferson had the first American recipe for ice cream. Modern versions of recipes enjoyed at Monticello are found in *Thomas Jefferson's Cook Book,* edited by Marie Kimball. The recipes use meats and fish that could be hunted, caught, or raised on Jefferson's plantation, plus all kinds of vegetables. Monticello cooks prepared pigeons, rabbit, mutton (sheep), chicken, ducks, and soups and many puddings. They also made pancakes, muffins, and custards.

Sugar's Cookies for the party

1¼ sticks soft butter

½ cup sugar

pinch of salt

1½ tsp. lemon extract

1 large fresh brown egg

2 cups all-purpose flour

Beat butter with electric mixer until creamy, then blend with sugar, salt, and egg. Add lemon extract and flour and stir until well-mixed. Refrigerate for four hours. Roll out flat and cut with cookie cutters. Place on parchment 1" apart on baking sheets and bake about 10 minutes.

Morse Code

Use the chart below to write in Morse code, or, go to http://www.onlineconversion.com/morse_code.htm for a fun instant translation. Bailey and her friends used this chart instead of the electronic version. There are more characters in code, including letters with accents, and punctuation symbols.

A ● —		N — ●
B — ● ● ●		O — — —
C — ● — ●		P ● — — ●
D — ● ●		Q — — ● —
E ●		R ● — ●
F ● ● — ●		S ● ● ●
G — — ●		T —
H ● ● ● ●		U ● ● —
I ● ●		V ● ● ● —
J ● — — —		W ● — —
K — ● —		X — ● ● —
L ● — ● ●		Y — ● — —
M — —		Z — — ● ●

Acknowledgments

Those who have helped shape this book are invaluable. Among them, Joseph Avent, Thomas Jefferson Foundation, Inc.; Jim Salisbury; Nancy Miller (for developing discussion questions); Abigail Grotke; Elizabeth Madden: Bert and Barbara Stafford; Hallie Vaughan; Dr. Lennart Johns; Julie Franklin; David Black; and as always, Amber. Mahalo.

About the Author

 Linda Salisbury draws her inspiration for the Bailey Fish Adventure series from her experiences in Florida and Virginia, and as a mother, grandmother, mentor, and foster mother.

Also in the Bailey Fish Adventure series are: *The Wild Women of Lake Anna,* a *ForeWord* magazine finalist for Book of the Year 2005; *No Sisters Sisters Club,* silver finalist in Florida Publishers Association's Best Children's Fiction 2008; *The Thief at Keswick Inn* (winner of the FPA, President's Pick Award 2007; *The Mysterious Jamestown Suitcase* (a bronze medalist in the Moonbeam Children's Book Awards); and *Ghost of the Chicken Coop Theater.* She's also the author of *Mudd Saves the Earth: Booger Glue, Cow Diapers and Other Good Ideas.*

About the Illustrator

 Illustrator and book designer Carol Tornatore lives in Nokomis, Florida, with her two Siamese cats. She has won numerous awards for her innovative book and magazine designs. Some of her other children's books include *Florida A to Z, The Runaway Bed, Zachary Cooks Up Some Fun*, and the *Southern Fossil Discovery* series. She enjoys going to the beach, collecting sea shells, and dancing.